A Brush with Magic

Also by William J. Brooke

A TELLING OF THE TALES
Five Stories

UNTOLD TALES

WILLIAM J. BROOKE

A Brush with Magic

based on a traditional Chinese story

illustrations by Michael Koelsch

HarperCollins*Publishers*

ĵ

Library of Congress Cataloging-in-Publication Data
Brooke, William J.
   A brush with magic; based on a traditional Chinese story / William J. Brooke ;
illustrations by Michael Koelsch.
      p.   cm.
   Summary: Liang, an orphan boy with a magic paintbrush that brings to life
whatever he paints, travels to the court of the Emperor of China to find his
fortune and true love.
   ISBN 0-06-022973-X. — ISBN 0-06-022974-8 (lib. bdg.)
   [1. Artists—Fiction.   2. Magic—Fiction.   3. China—Fiction.]   I. Koelsch, Michael, ill.   II.
Title.
PZ7.B78977Br   1993   92-41744
[Fic]—dc20   CIP
                                                                                         AC

Typography by Al Cetta
1   2   3   4   5   6   7   8   9   10
❖
First Edition

To Joyce (whose idea it was)
and Patrick Stoner
Friends for
So Long
and to Lynne
Friend for
Ever

Magic is not as simple as it looks.
A man once found an old clay
pot. He put a little water and rice
into it and went to get firewood, but
when he came back the water was already boiling.

"It is a magic cookpot!" he exclaimed, and
showed it to his neighbors. Again he put in water
and rice, and the meal was ready in moments. He
offered to let them use it for a price, but they
laughed at him. The trees grew thick on the hill-
sides there, and firewood was the only thing they
had in abundance. This was magic, certainly, but
what was the value of it?

The man was determined to get some value out
of the magic. At night, he lay on his pallet and
imagined what he could do with wealth and power.
By day, he watched the pot bubbling, and his
wishes boiled up like water with no rice to go in it.

At last, a merchant from a distant city where
wood was scarce offered a piece of silver for the

1

pot. The man was sorry to get no more, yet so pleased to get anything that he rubbed the silver between his hands with glee. The merchant was sorry to pay at all, yet so pleased it didn't cost more that he rubbed the pot between his hands with glee. A genie appeared from the pot and offered to grant him whatever wishes he might make.

"Anything?" asked the merchant, while the man looked on in shock.

"Yes," said the genie. "Just as long as you don't pour in any more water and rice. This pot is my home, and I hate sharing it with another man's dinner."

"It makes you angry?" the man asked timidly.

The genie narrowed his eyes at him. "It makes me boil!" he said.

Magic is seldom what it seems.

O N E

"You have the gift," said the sweet, familiar voice, as tiny hands reached up from the basket to receive the brush. "Use it well." There was a flash of steel in bright sunlight, and the basket splashed down into the swift current of the river.

It is strange that we call a river by a single name when it is so many different things. This river was born high in the mountains, mingled of pure springs and rainwater to blend into a freshet, then a brook, then a stream. It plunged with youthful daring into a gorge and dashed exultantly between the walls, flinging its spray high in the air. It slowed as it reached the lowlands, as the first few dwellings of humans appeared, then began to cluster, then to crowd, then to strangle it. Beneath rotten piers and overhanging shanties, it became a creeping blackness, clogged with filth from the commerce of humankind. But, slow and sure, it survived even that. It broadened out, slowed further, and finally became a stately green procession through wide, lush valleys where rice paddies huddled close like avid students determined to catch the least word murmured by an aged but well-honored teacher.

In such a valley, a poor farmer named Li was talking to the tender rice shoots as he waded among them, cleaning and weeding. "The rains have been good to you this year. You are green and beautiful. I must tend you carefully, for you are many happy suppers to come."

Li raised his head to wipe sweat from his forehead. Stooping in the hot sun was hard work. He glanced about, then wiped his eyes as well, unsure of what he saw. There was a basket afloat in the river. A slow current brought it near the bank.

"What could it be?" he nervously asked the tender rice shoots, which did not answer. The question was important to him. Li's life was an unvarying routine that might have seemed boring to someone else. But it was the unchanging sameness of it that protected him, like a forest creature whose coloring blends it into the jungle and hides it from the eaters that watch. Li's life was surrounded by dangers, and the slightest change might call their attention and destroy him. Not enough sun, too much sun, not enough rain, too much rain, many different paths all led to starvation. In such a world, the wise man avoided the unforeseen and planned no further than the next meal.

The basket floated close to Li and hesitated in a slight eddy. "Well, you seem to be waiting for me," he said, "so there's no use in pretending I don't see you. When luck chooses you, there's no use asking if it's a rope of gold or a tiger's tail. You just have to grab tight and hope for the best." So he finally stepped down into the river and caught up the basket in his arms. When he placed it on the bank, it opened outward and disclosed its contents.

"A baby!" he cried to the river. "Could you have brought me any worse luck? I can barely feed myself, much less a baby. If I keep him, his luck will be even worse than mine. Yet I can't toss him back into you like a fish too small for the keeping. Oh, what to do!"

The child was more than an infant but not yet of the age to talk. He nevertheless made his feelings abundantly clear by letting loose a great tearful howl. Li was horrified that such a small body could produce such a quantity of sound. "It's hungry," he said to the rice paddy, which still pretended not to hear him. He grabbed up the child and its blanket and hurried to his hut a little back from the river's edge among the trees. He built up the fire and warmed the bit of rice and fish meant for his supper and set it before the little boy. The crying did not diminish. "No, of course it can't eat you," he said to the rice. "It's not old enough. It needs milk, but there is only one goat in the village, and I have nothing to trade for milk. Oh, why did it have to wash up just here?"

Li looked through the damp blanket wrapping the child for anything that might help. There was nothing but a stick with bristles on one end. He had never seen a paintbrush before, but it looked to him like what the scribe three villages away used to write letters for people. He examined it curiously, rubbing the smoothness of the wood and touching the softness of the bristles to his face. He did not notice that the child stopped crying and reached a greedy hand toward the brush.

"Well," Li said to the paintbrush, "pleasant as you are, you will be of no use around here except as kindling." He set it with the bits of wood next to the fire. Instantly, the child began to wail, louder than ever.

Li waved his hands in confusion. He was used to talking to all the inanimate things in his life and was perfectly happy never being answered. Now he was getting more response in an hour than he usually got in a year. He went out into his little yard and spoke to a tree. "If I only had a goat to give it some milk." The tree didn't answer, which made Li feel better.

When Li walked away, the child squirmed out of his blanket and crawled and scrambled until he had the brush in his hand. His tears stopped at once. The feel of the brush had always been his pacifier.

Through the open arch of the door, he could see the funny old man talking about goats and milk, which meant nothing to him. But then the old man half consciously moved his hands in the gesture of milking a goat. This made a picture in the child's head, and the picture made his mouth water. Words meant nothing to him, but pictures were powerful in his mind.

He raised the brush before his eyes, holding it not as an infant thoughtlessly clasps a stick, but as if some power flowed from it into his hand, giving him a sense of purpose beyond his age. He rubbed the brush in the black ash of the fire, then crawled to a spot where the mud plaster of the wall had been bleached white by sunlight pouring through the doorway. He braced himself against the wall and shoved upward on tottering feet. When he was standing shakily, he smiled and extended the brush in a steady and confident hand toward the smooth whiteness.

Li finished explaining the situation to the tree and noticed the crying had stopped. He went inside to find the child making black marks on the wall. He had been fond of that wall, often speaking to the pleasant blankness that was now a mess of criss-crossing lines. Well, not a mess. They were actually quite orderly. Four sets of lines like legs, a big oval, a smaller circle with little things like horns. As he looked, the lines began to remind him of something.

He shook his head. "A man won't get anything practical accomplished," he explained to the paintbrush as he took it from the child, "if he wastes his time figuring out what a bunch of lines on a wall looks like." The fire was beginning to die down, so he tossed the brush onto it as he would any other bit of a stick.

The child gave a wail and tried to reach right into the flames. Li pulled him back, but he kept struggling forward, so the old man finally grabbed the brush out and returned it, mildly singed, to the child. Li went back out to the tree. "The damage is already done to the wall," he explained. "And if I can't feed him, at least this keeps him quiet."

"Bah!" barked the tree, much to Li's surprise. He wasn't sure how to answer, but then there was another "Bah!" and he realized it came from behind him. He turned to see a black-and-white goat, bleating where it stood in his doorway.

Li stared in amazement. He looked around for the goat's owner, but there was no one. Finally he fetched a rope and tied the goat to the doorpost. He milked it into a little bowl and gave it to the child, who drank messily and happily splashed his brush in the spilled milk.

Li watched all this with interest. When the milk was gone, he washed the bowl in the river and fetched water to wash the wall. But the wall was white and clean as before. The lines and circles were gone. Li looked at the wall, at the goat, at the child. Then he went to talk to the tree.

"Either the goat wandered in here on its own, which is a great stroke of good fortune, or the hairy stick is a magic stick, which might be good fortune or bad. Or both." He was silent in thought for a while. The tree said nothing.

"I shall be grateful that the goat wandered in here on its own," he finally decided. "When a good thing happens to you, you can worry about why or how or where from, until the thing gets bored and walks away. Or you can just accept it and go on."

The child made a sound. He was smiling as he brushed at the ground.

"I believe he said 'Li,'" the old man informed the tree. "Or perhaps it was 'Pa.' Or maybe it was nothing at all." He looked hard at the tree and suddenly realized that it bored him.

Knees creaking, he lowered himself into the dust by the laughing child. Li felt something strange about his face, an unaccustomed twisting of the muscles. It was a smile.

"I'll call you Liang," he said.

T W O

"Liang!" called Li from the rice paddy. Seven years had passed.

A year is like a river. It is called by a single name or number, yet every day and even every second of it is different for every person who lives through it. In a wide, green valley, a year can move as slowly and changelessly as a wide, green river. Or a year can come boiling out of the equinox like a river at flood. A year can bring you good or bad, and you learn which only by living it, just as a river can bring you a basket and you discover what's within only by opening it.

"Liang!" Li called again. This time Liang heard and appeared from down the river, brush in hand. He grabbed a rake and carried it to Li. "No! I want the hoe, not the rake. Where did you wander off to, and what was on your mind? Ha, what is ever on your mind?"

"Well," answered Liang, "I found some nice yellow mud, so I made a picture of a beautiful goldfish. And I tried to bring it for you to see, but it gasped so terribly that I had to put it in the river, and it swam away."

"You are hopeless," Li told him. "All your foolish talk of pictures coming to life. I have tried you at every task on the farm, but your mind always wanders to that useless stick. I am sorry I did not burn it when you were a baby."

Liang ignored this old familiar song. Li had never believed, almost as if he didn't *want* to believe in the magic of the brush, which made no sense to Liang. Rather than try yet again to convince him, Liang said, "Tell me about my parents."

Li sighed. "I have told you more times than there are grains of rice in the paddies. I know nothing of your parents. You were in a basket with that foolish stick and nothing else."

"But did it look as if the basket got in the river by accident or deliberately? Was I wrapped up carefully or just shoved into it? Were there any marks on it?"

"I don't remember! They took the time to put in that hairy stick. That is all I can say about them."

"I dreamed of them again last night," Liang said. "I'm sure of it! I wish I could remember the dreams. I only know I wake up happy because they were there."

Li scowled. "Go play in the woods and leave me to my work."

Liang wandered sadly into the forest. Why did being told to do the very thing he wanted to do make him feel so bad? He looked back at the familiar figure of Li bent to his work. Why was the old man so mean to him sometimes?

As Liang watched unseen, Li stopped to wipe away the sweat. No, Liang realized, it wasn't his forehead Li mopped, it was his eyes. Why would he cry?

"Does it hurt him that I want to talk about my parents when he asks for my help?" He felt a swell of affection in his heart for this old man who worked so hard to provide for the two of them, and he determined to do something nice for Li. He would try again to help with the rice! But, no, he was so bad at that, it would just depress and irritate Li even more.

Suddenly the idea came of drawing a picture for Li, a picture of Li himself. Surely he would enjoy that!

Liang spread mud on a rock. He thought of all the lines on Li's face and the straggly white eyebrows sticking out every which way, and he laughed at the funny old face. But as he pictured it, he felt without thinking the warmth of the fond glances those eyes gave him when they weren't squinted against sun and sweat. And even as he laughed, to his mind's eye the face of Li was beautiful. He began to etch it into the mud.

It took only a few quick strokes for the likeness to appear. Then he began to add shading, scraping away mud to allow the darker rock to show through. It was surprising how a few lines made the face seem to swell outward until it looked as if Li himself were hidden in the rock, just putting his face out for a look around. But as Liang was finishing the few wisps of hair, he was distracted by the chittering of a monkey in a tree.

"Oh, ho," he said, "you don't like my picture. You think you could do better. Or perhaps you don't like the subject matter. You would prefer a picture of yourself." With a laugh he quickly sketched in the body of a monkey below Li's head. "There!" he said as he finished. "Do you like that better? I shall call it Monk-Li," he said with a laugh.

He stared at the picture. The eyes looked back at him disapprovingly. "What is wrong?" he asked. "I have finished you, yet you just sit there. Why do you not come to life?" He laughed. "I see. Your tale cannot begin until I finish your tail." He quickly added a few lines for the missing tail.

With a bound, Monk-Li swelled out from the rock and leaped into a tree.

The real monkey fled in surprise and fear, making his gibbering noises all the way. "Wait!" called Monk-Li after it. "That is, I mean to say . . ." And he screwed up his little Li face and attempted to gibber, but it just sounded silly, like an embarrassed grown-up trying to make monkey noises.

Liang laughed loudly. "It's very well for you to laugh," said Monk-Li, "but what am I supposed to do? If the monkeys will have nothing to do with me, what are the chances that I'll be accepted by a bunch of humans?"

"You are the first drawing that ever talked back to me," Liang said. "I'm used to my pictures running or flying or swimming away, but I'm not used to them standing up and complaining. I don't think I like it."

"You shouldn't have finished me if you didn't want me to stand up, and you shouldn't have given me Li's head if you didn't want me to complain. I'm hungry. Give me a banana."

"Come down here," Liang ordered. "Come down and stop your chattering, and you'll get your banana." Monk-Li came down slowly as Liang began to draw a banana.

"You could make it bigger," suggested Monk-Li.

"Or a whole bunch! And no black spots and all nice and ripe."

When Monk-Li got within reach, quick as a wink, Liang brushed some mud over the mouth of the surprised monkey. In a moment, the mouth was gone and there was nothing but smooth, blank skin between his nose and his chin. He leaped back into the tree and mumbled "Mmm! Mmm!" down at the boy, who doubled up with laughter.

"You look so funny!" The monkey tried to appear dignified and very offended. It was hard to look tight-lipped without a mouth, but he did a commendable job of it. "Come," said Liang, "don't be upset. It was just a joke. And you brought it on yourself by talking so much. Here, this is for you." He finished the banana and stepped back.

Monk-Li climbed down slowly, suspiciously, then darted forward to grab the banana. Without thinking, he zipped it open and thrust it into his mouth. Or where his mouth had been. It squashed messily against the blankness there. Liang laughed even louder at Monk-Li's expression with its mixture of squashed banana and disgust.

"I am sorry," called Liang, trying not to laugh. "I know this is bad of me, but sometimes I just have to laugh at things. Come down, no more tricks, I'll fix your mouth." The monkey came-back slowly.

Liang sketched a new mouth into the yellow squash of banana. Monk-Li flexed his new lips this way and that, experimenting. He started to say something, but Liang shook a warning finger at him, so he kept quiet and ate instead.

"Liang!" called Li from down by the river.

"Uncle Li!" Liang called back to him. "Come see what I've done for you! Do come! You'll be very pleased!"

Li puffed up the pathway from the riverbank and looked around. "What are you talking about?"

Liang pointed, but Monk-Li was gone. He looked around. "Up there!" he said.

Li looked. "It's just a monkey." He looked closer. "A very ugly monkey."

"I drew him for you. He has your face and he can talk. Come, Monk-Li, say something." Monk-Li smiled down and made unlikely monkey sounds. "Oh, don't be angry, just say some little thing. Really, Uncle Li, he was talking like anything a minute ago."

Li was staring at the monkey. "I don't look anything like that!" he said. "Now stop this nonsense. I have a job for you. While I go into the village to trade for some fish, I want you to keep the birds out of the rice. Just wave your arms and shout now and then. Even you can do that, I think."

"Of course I can," said Liang, hurt by both Li's low opinion and Monk-Li's silence.

Li left and Liang, after a few insulting remarks to the monkey, wandered down to the rice paddies, where the birds were already nibbling at the tender shoots. "Hi-yah!" Liang yelled and leaped into the air, flailing his arms.

The birds looked surprised and flew off a short distance. Liang felt very proud of himself. He strutted around, pounding his chest, announcing his fearsomeness. The birds watched and listened and then flew back into the paddy.

"Hey!" yelled Liang. And "Hey-yah!" And "Please!" The birds moved, but not far. This was harder than it looked.

Liang saw some children running along the path above the paddies that led to the village. "Why are you running?" he called, glad to be distracted.

"The great Court Painter is resting in the village, and we are going to see him," said a little girl.

"What is a painter?" asked Liang.

Some of the children laughed at that. "A painter makes drawings of things," said the little girl.

"I do that," Liang said brightly. "I draw things with my magic stick, and they come to life. I drew a monkey just this morning. He is in the trees over there, but he refuses to talk."

The girl laughed at that. "The Court Painter is

much better than your silly imaginings. His pictures are called Art, and I am told they don't look anything like real life, which must be very hard to do."

"I wish I could go see them," said Liang, "but I have been given the important job of frightening the birds." Just then, one of the birds landed on his shoulder and pecked curiously at his hair. He shoved it away and jumped up and down, yelling with embarrassment.

The girl laughed again. "Put up a scarecrow. You know, some old clothes on a few sticks. It would have to be more frightening than you."

"Oh, sure, I'll do that," Liang said, ashamed to admit that the only clothes he and Li owned were on their backs. When the children were gone, Liang looked after them longingly. But the birds were already creeping back. What could he do?

It suddenly struck him what would frighten the birds more than a few old clothes on sticks. He ignored the birds and began to scrape with his brush at the mud of the riverbank.

The first thing he sketched was a foot. A big foot. With three toes. And razor-sharp claws.

And it was covered with scales.

T H R E E

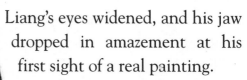

Liang's eyes widened, and his jaw dropped in amazement at his first sight of a real painting.

A painting is like a river. It is many things in one, and each person who looks at it sees something different. Perhaps because in puddle or painting, the thoughtful gaze discovers its own reflection.

The colors! Reds and golds and blues and greens, plus colors of which he had only dreamed. And all on a sheet of paper, a material he had never seen before. The thought of something that existed only to be drawn on was amazing to someone who had drawn only on rock and mud and dirt.

He flipped through more of the drawings. Each new picture made him gasp in joy and envy. And they stayed right there, flat on the page! No leaping into the trees for these drawings. Of course, they did not actually look much like the things they showed. Everything was flat and stiff, and the people showed no sense of who they were in their faces. Perhaps that was the secret of Art: To keep it in its place you had to make sure it didn't look like anything.

Beside the pictures, he found a box and a brush. The brush was like his, except not as worn and ragged. He opened the box. It was full of color. All the rainbow hues of the pictures laid out in neat rows. He could not remember having seen paints, but a picture came into his mind from long before, and he knew what they were.

A horse whinnied outside. Liang looked cautiously around the room. The Court Painter was dining with the village elders, so Liang had slipped into the house that had been put at his disposal. Thick pillows were thrown about for reclining, and fine clothes spilled out of the saddlebags, which sparkled with brass and silver in a corner. He was startled for a moment to see someone else, but then he realized that it was his own reflection. He had never seen a mirror before, but he had seen himself bent over in the still puddles of the rice paddies. He liked his reflection better standing up.

He took out his magic stick and dipped the

wooden end of it into the paint, the way he would have scratched in the mud. He made a mark on the back of one of the drawings. It thrilled him, but it wasn't quite right. He dipped the brush end into the paint and made a mark. The handle had made a hard line. The brush made a soft one, feathering off at the end, showing the touch of each bristle. It was so much finer than his mud strokes could ever be!

Liang was enraptured. The blank sheet seemed to cry out for the paint. He looked around impatiently for a subject, and there was the mirror. He had never given a thought before to how he looked, but now his image passed through his eyes into his mind and down his arm into the brush, and he found himself, without thinking about it, beautiful.

He painted himself painting, his face, his clothes, his hands. The look in the eyes brightened with joy as he moved toward the feet that would complete the picture. The grasp of the painted hand tightened on the brush, and the picture looked ready to leap out and draw the world.

"What are you doing?" shouted a man as he grabbed the paint box from Liang's hand.

Liang was startled, but still flushed with excitement. From the fine clothes, this must be the

Court Painter and he would surely understand Liang's feeling. "I'm making a picture," he said, gesturing to the painting, which lost its spark and settled back onto the page, just a few strokes short of life.

The Court Painter started to scold the boy, then looked closer at the picture. He had almost imagined a movement . . . Never mind. The picture had none of the proper characteristics of portraiture, yet it was well sketched, even lifelike, if one cared for that sort of thing.

"Do you like my drawing?" Liang asked timidly.

The Court Painter pulled himself together. It was bad enough that one had to endure plain dinners of fish and rice and the boring conversation of country folk, without finding someone handling your belongings. Still, one depended on the hospitality of these peasants when traveling, so one mustn't offend. At least until after they had provided breakfast tomorrow. Remain superior yet pleasant. "Your drawing? It has no sense of style, the color is drab, and the pose lacks metaphoric significance."

"But don't you think it looks like me?"

The Painter waved at the mirror. "*That* looks like you. A painting must display Art, not likeness. It must reveal inner meanings that do not show in simple anatomy. To begin with, I would never paint a simple peasant boy. That is an inappropriate subject for Art. Here, let us suppose you are a great warrior, a member of the Imperial Guard." With quick strokes of his own brush, he painted a sword over the brush in the picture and stiff leather armor over the loose and ragged clothing. In moments, the body became flat where it had been rounded before and frozen where it had seemed about to move. Only the face of Liang remained, and the joy and beauty of it stood out starkly above the rest of the painting.

"Now, the face will require the traditional warrior's grimace—an expression, I might add modestly, for which my Art has always been justly acclaimed."

"I understand," said Liang, depressed, pushing the picture away before the Painter could correct the face. How difficult Art is, Liang thought, this ability to look at something and then paint it in a way that looks nothing like it. Out loud he said, "I could never be an Artist." The Painter was pleased that the boy had realized the immense superiority of his own ability.

Liang turned the picture over so he would not have to look at his failure. He caught his breath. He had not looked before at the picture on the back. It showed a girl about his own age brushing the hair of another girl who sat at a rich dressing table. "Who is this?" asked Liang, filled with wonder at the beauty of the girl who stood brushing the other's hair.

"The Princess," the Painter answered, "the first daughter of the Emperor, who is my master." He was looking only at the seated girl whose hair was being brushed. As an important member of the Court, he made a point of ignoring servants except to give commands or reprimands. That was why this picture had been a failure and never presented to the Princess. He had been so struck by the beauty of the little servant girl, who was supposed to be mere decoration in the picture, that he had accidentally painted a fair likeness of her.

"The Princess," breathed Liang. "She is beautiful." He forced himself to look away from her. His eye passed quickly over the stiff figure seated at the table. "What are those bumps back there outside the window?"

"Bumps? Where? Those? Those are mountains, of course!"

"Then these must be—"

"Trees!"

"I was going to guess that," said Liang, who felt he was getting better at Art recognition. The things were tall and spindly and looked like some sort of drying rack, so they must be trees. Of course, recognizing them was one thing, painting them was quite another. He would never be able to look at a mountain or a tree and paint anything like this at all.

"Where is this place?" he asked, holding up another picture, bright with golds and reds and yellows.

"That is the Court of the Emperor."

"And you live there and are rich and all because of your Art?"

"Yes," the Court Painter said with satisfaction. Under his influence, the boy was learning to appreciate the finer things.

"I wish I could go there," Liang sighed, thinking of the beautiful Princess.

The Painter laughed. "You have no gift for Art," he said, "and without money you will never get to Court."

"Money," said Liang. He had heard of that. But, like Art, he had never seen any before.

"Do all of your pictures stay so nicely on the page?" he asked.

"You mean my use of space and the relationship of the figures to the frame?"

"No. I mean do they ever jump off the page and shout insults at you from the trees?"

This was an area of artistic discussion which the

Court Painter had never encountered before. After a pause, which was mostly spent deciding that Liang wasn't big enough to present any real threat, he said definitely, "No, a drawing is not alive. Art is Art and life is life and the two have nothing to do with each other."

"My pictures come to life!" Liang said eagerly. "It is because of my magic brush."

"Yes, no doubt," the Painter replied indulgently, eyeing the straggly brush in the boy's hand. "That is what we call a 'figment of the imagination.' It means you think it happens, but it doesn't really. A drawing cannot come to life. Magic has nothing to do with Art. Art is created by great learning, much practice, and close following of the rules. All that requires money. And now it is time for you to go."

Once the boy was gone, the Court Painter looked at the picture of the Princess, which was ruined now by the boy's drawing on the back. He started to tear it up, then paused. Perhaps he would give it to the little servant girl when he returned to Court. It never hurt to be on good terms with those who are close to the nobility. He rolled it carefully and put it in his saddlebag.

Liang walked down the path with many thoughts in his head. How to get to the Court? How to meet the Princess? It seemed impossible,

and yet nothing else mattered. If he could not live among those colors, why live at all?

Monk-Li swung out of a tree onto his shoulder. "I'm hungry," he said. "Give me a banana."

"I'm not talking to you. You're not real. I have it on the best authority that all my drawings are just figments."

Monk-Li shrugged. "If you don't have a banana, I suppose a figment would do."

"I need money. You are a drawing and there's no money in drawings. Especially ones with big appetites." He tossed the monkey back up into the trees.

"Please," called the little voice, "don't joke anymore with me. Here I am, neither monkey nor human, and you're responsible. I'm just a thing you drew to amuse yourself."

"Well, you don't amuse me," Liang called back. "And you are *not* my responsibility. It was the magic brush that brought you to life. It's not my fault." He felt a little bad, but he reminded himself that Monk-Li was an impossibility according to the Court Painter, who was much more knowledgeable in such matters. Still, Liang supposed he could spare the time to imagine a few more figments to feed the little monkey, even if he didn't exist.

He was just turning back when he heard,

"Liang! You are completely irresponsible!"

"Monk-Li," he answered, "I never—" But he got no further than that when Li's hand fell on his shoulder.

"What did you call me?"

"My Uncle Li," said Liang, embarrassed. "I just said it fast, like 'M'Unc'Li.'"

Li pulled him down the path. "Well, you'd better do some more fast talking to explain why you left the rice unattended."

"But I didn't," said Liang quickly. "I drew a much better guardian than . . ." He fell silent as he thought what the Court Painter would say to that.

"You drew?" demanded Li. "You drew something to protect the rice? Oh, Liang, when will you learn that drawings are foolishness but rice is our very lives."

"I *have* learned that," Liang answered as they arrived at the riverbank by the rice paddies. "Just today. No more drawing for me."

"I wish I could believe that," Li muttered, looking around. "Well, we are in luck. The birds have left the rice alone. No thanks to this drawing of yours, wherever it is."

"You're standing on it," said Liang.

Li looked and jumped into the air. He made a good effort not to come down again, but eventually he had to.

It was a dragon. A great fire-breather, with terrible claws and scales and big burning eyes. "I drew it flat and didn't finish it, so it wouldn't run away," Liang explained. "I just made it real enough to scare the birds."

Liang stopped, embarrassed at the hopeless way Li was looking at him. Yet the thought came unbidden of how much grander he could make the dragon if he just had some paints. Instead of flat mud browns and yellows, gold for the scales, green frills, red eyes . . .

He made himself stop. "I really have learned, Uncle Li." He took the paint stick out of his pocket and looked at it sadly. Then he threw it far away into the tangle of forest.

Li smiled in happy surprise. "Have you really learned some sense?"

"Yes," said Liang. "No more figments for me. From now on, my only purpose is to get to the Court!"

Li's smile ceased abruptly, and he shook his head sadly at this new madness.

"Tell me about money," said Liang.

F O U R

If there'd just been some money, she could have hired a horse and left her fears far behind. But all she possessed was wrapped in a poor, tiny bundle as she hurried on foot along the path, flinching at every imagined noise that pursued her.

A pathway is like a year, carrying us through space rather than time. Choosing a path is choosing the future. A path is always its own opposite. It leads both to and away: to a friend or work or food or a new chance; away from home or a loved one or a failed opportunity. It is hope and it is despair, depending which way you face. All the possibility of a path could drown you surely as a river.

For this particular young woman, this particular path led away. Away from oppression, away from fear. Yet fear crowded close on her heels, and she could never run fast enough to follow the pathway to hope.

She clutched her little bundle. Through the cloth, she could feel the crinkle of a rolled-up piece of paper. Even in her fear, she smiled at that touch. This precious paper had been a gift, a bribe really, seven years before. It held two pictures, one on each side. One of the pictures was engraved in her memory. The other picture, which she never gave more than a glance, showed two girls, one seated, one standing with a brush.

She had scarcely paused during her days of flight, and she looked thirstily at the wide, green river below the path. She could imagine the sound of hoofbeats behind her, yet she must drink. She went into the high, concealing weeds on the bank near the rice paddies and cleared a space to kneel for a drink.

Instead, she screamed.

Clapping muddy hands over her mouth to stifle the unwanted shriek, she scrambled back into the undergrowth. Perhaps no one had heard! But there were sounds of movement in the weeds. Someone was really there! Before she could gather herself to flee, the weeds parted and the face of Liang appeared.

She gasped. Without thinking, her hand

touched again the paper in her bundle. It was the face from the picture, seven years older but still somehow the same. It was the face that was her only consolation, the face to which she confided everything. She looked into the face she thought of as her only friend.

Liang looked into *her* face and burst out laughing.

"Sorry," he said, "I don't mean to laugh, but your face is a mess. Let's clean you up here."

She felt the mud on her face then and smiled weakly as he reached out a hand to her. She took it and let him lead her toward the bank, then pulled back abruptly, pointing at the ground. Liang laughed again. There, peering out from among the weeds, was the head of his old dragon scarecrow.

"Is that what frightened you?" he asked. He pulled up more of the weeds to reveal the claws and the scales. "That's just a silly old thing that I drew years ago."

"It looks very real!" she said. She did not want him to think she was frightened by every little thing.

He regarded it critically. "I suppose it's not bad," he agreed. "I was really a very good sketcher, but I knew nothing about Art and there was no money to be had in just drawing things, so I quit."

"Is money the only reason to draw things?"

"Money is the thing that will get me to the Court and the Prin . . . well, other things as well. All the things that are really important in life."

"I have seen some Art, and it never impressed me. But I like a drawing that looks like some-thing." She gazed into his face and had one partic-ular drawing in mind.

"You thought this was real?" He gestured to the remains of the dragon.

"Yes, for a moment."

He didn't want to waste important time with foolishness, but there was something about this girl that made him enjoy her attention. There was something familiar about her, too. Without think-ing, he blurted out something he hadn't thought of in years.

"I used to think that my drawings came to life and talked to me. When I was little, I mean." He was instantly sorry he had said it. Now she would laugh at him.

She looked at the dragon and then at him. "*Did* they come to life?"

Was she making fun of him? But she looked at him so seriously, he could not think it was a joke. "I *thought* they did," he replied, trying to decide what was so familiar about her. "I had a magic brush that my parents had given me, and it made my drawings . . ." He stopped and gave himself a shake. "But, of course, that's ridiculous, so I quit drawing and started to . . ."

"Started to what?" she asked when he broke off.

Liang hesitated. He had no experience of young women. There had been girls his age in the village, but they refused to listen to stories of magic paint-brushes. Now they were all married and raising families and tending their paddies, and he was re-garded as crazy and useless. But this young woman looked at him with interest, her eyes peering brightly from her muddy face. He liked talking to her, although it scared him a little, too.

"Come, I'll show you," he said, holding out his hand.

She reached happily for his hand, but a sound on the path froze her in terror. "They're here!" she gasped.

But it was only an old black-and-white goat. Liang caught him by the horns. "Don't mind him. He eats through his rope and goes for walks around . . . Hey! Where did you go?" he asked the empty spot where she had been.

After a moment, there was a rustling in the depths of the reeds. "Why, what's that moving down there?" asked Liang, pretending to be frightened. "Is it my dragon come to life?"

"Stop being silly," she said, standing and brushing dirt and twigs from her clothes.

"Who is looking for you that you're so frightened?"

"For me?" she asked, with an unconvincing laugh. "No one is looking for me. Goats make me nervous, that's all. I'm just a poor peasant girl on my way to my aunt's village downriver." She gestured vaguely.

"Well, if you need a place to stay tonight, there's an empty hut where you could be quite alone, just . . . downriver." He smiled and pointed casually in the opposite direction from her gesture. "In case someone were looking for you, which I know they're not." She looked so irritated with herself at being found out so easily that he had to laugh again. "Now, tell me, O Hider-in-the-Reeds, do you have a name?"

"Of course I do. My name is Lotus."

"Lotus. That's a pretty name. You're not from around here. They don't bother much with pretty names here, or pretty anything, for that matter. If it's no use in the fields, they pay it no attention."

"But not you? Are you such a great lover of beauty?"

"A lover of money. I look far beyond this valley."

"And what is your name, O Seer-of-Distant-Gold?"

"Liang. A plain name, I know, but well suited to such phrases as 'Liang the Mighty,' 'Liang the All-Powerful' and, of course, 'Liang the Incredibly Wealthy.'" She had to laugh at that, and he joined her with good nature.

"You were going to show me something."

He was suddenly nervous, wanting her to be impressed by his work, feeling it somehow important that she approve of him. He had to admit that no one else did.

In the years since his encounter with the Court Painter, Liang had first tried to be such a good farmer that there would be surplus to sell for money. He did everything Li told him, but it never made sense to him and he was bored and no good at it. Healthy plants turned yellow under his closest care. He watched Li tending and coaxing and urging the rice to its full growth, and it seemed a form of magic to him.

When Liang came up with his first money-making scheme, Li was happy to get him out of his way. Liang devoted himself for weeks to building a ferry across the river. When it sank, he tried a floating toll bridge. He gave up when Li pointed out there was no difference between the two sides of the river, so why would anyone pay to cross? Turning to smaller schemes, Liang invented ingenious labor-saving devices that somehow managed to double the time and effort required to carry out a chore.

Li became once again accustomed to working alone. But each failed attempt made Liang more determined. He was convinced that, any invention now, he would become fabulously rich and go to the Court and marry the Princess. As he took Lotus' hand now, she suddenly seemed almost to look like the remembered face of the Princess. The thought made him laugh. He compared the rich colors of the painting and the drab little creature before him. Pretty, perhaps. Striking, even, but hardly a Princess.

He led her with one hand through the trees and undergrowth, dragging the goat with the other. Pushing aside some bushes, he announced, "Here it is!" and gestured with pride to a contraption of bamboo and buckets alongside the river.

"It's very elaborate," she said cautiously, "but what is it?"

"It's a sure-fire irrigation assembly. You see, I tie the goat here and he turns the wheel there, and the buckets get pulled up and carried over there to where they dump the water and circle around under to get more, while the water runs down the bamboo pipes to the . . ." He stopped when he saw Lotus shaking her head.

"Look, it's simple," insisted Liang, but he felt a little confused himself. "Here." He grabbed a stick and squatted in the mud by the river. A few quick strokes made it all clear.

"Now, watch it work," said Liang. "I was just about to try it for the first time when I was interrupted by a scream of appreciation from a very outspoken Art critic." Lotus giggled at that.

Liang attached a branch to a harness so that tender leaves dangled just before the goat's eager mouth. It began to caper forward, turning the wheel. There was a sloshing sound, and the first bucket of water began to rise.

"You see!" cried Liang happily. Lotus found her eye drawn more to his face than to his clattering machine. It glowed now in the delight of its creation, just like the face in her picture.

The bucket rose and dangled through the air, and for a moment it looked as if it would work. Then the bucket lurched and emptied, not into a pipe, but onto the shaky foundations of the machine itself. Liang jumped forward to make adjustments, but the next bucket spilled onto the goat, startling it out of its usual plod and into a scamper.

More buckets flipped, drenching Liang and the dirt around the bamboo uprights. Lotus rushed to help and was immediately soaked.

"Grab that!" shouted Liang, but before she could tell what he meant, there was a creaking groan and the whole contraption keeled over and sank into the mud. They watched in silence as the goat chewed happily at the splintered bamboo of the wreck.

"It almost worked," said Lotus.

Liang sighed. "But it didn't. They never do. They're useless. Just like me, just like everyone says I am." Lotus reached out for him, but he shook his head and stepped away, not knowing how to accept her sympathy. "It's all right. I'm used to it. That hut is just there along the path." He tried to smile. "You'll be safe from whatever isn't following you."

That made her turn her eyes fearfully behind her, and when she turned back he had slipped away. She sighed deeply and went to look for the hut.

Only the goat was left to hear the faint whir and splash at the riverbank, on the very spot where Liang had drawn in the mud. It trotted over to investigate and found a tiny duplicate of Liang's invention busily carrying water in a most efficient manner. For a moment it admired the thin bamboo arms rising and turning and carrying the lacy wickerwork of tiny baskets, then showed its appreciation for the delicate mechanism by nibbling it down to the mud.

F I V E

Arms moving this way and that in the flailing stroke of an uncertain swimmer, Liang tossed on his pallet bed.

Night comes like a gentle flood. Darkness fills the hollows of earth and rises gradually higher until, with a rush, it covers the highest trees and the mountaintops. Only then does it reveal its stars, sparkling like sunglints on water. Just as people cannot breathe the essence of the flood, their waking selves cannot bear the stuff of night, which is dream. When they lie awake in the dark, they are filled with night terror, with blindness, with cold and anguish. But asleep! Asleep, they plunge into dream like seals waddling from arid shores to slide joyously into slippery green depth.

The body plods, but the soul is a swimmer.

In this particular night, Liang ranged far and wide through the flood of dream. He escaped the little bit of village and riverbank which was all he knew by day, and roved time and space with casual backstrokes. He saw the Princess, her back turned, but undoubtedly the Princess because of her beautiful robes of gold and scarlet. Then she turned and her face had streaks of mud and looked like . . . But he gave a kick and swam away. Something there did not fit his plans, and so he chose not to see.

He was somewhere else and very small. Hands held him, hurried but loving. He heard a terrible voice saying, "We can't hang the painting, so we'll hang the painter." He felt the rough weave of a basket beneath him. Something was thrust into his hands. A paintbrush! Was he the painter to be hanged? The awful voice echoed in his ears, but another voice spoke quietly and drove it away. "You have the gift," it said. "Use it well."

"My father," thought Liang in the unthinking wisdom of sleep. "It is the voice of my father. Why can I not see him?"

Liang tried to stay there, floating in that moment, but he was so light-headed with joy that he shot to the surface and burst into the gray light creeping through his little window. It took several moments for dream to seep away into the soil of reality; then he looked down at his hand. It clutched a paintbrush. A little box of paints was beside the pallet where he slept.

"My father's gift!" he said with wonder. But that other voice from his dream still echoed harshly in his ear. Who was it? Who would hang the painter?

Night had brought neither sleep nor dream to Lotus. She was too heavy with thought and fear to float. But for the first time since her flight from the Court, thought outweighed fear.

Liang. There was much she liked about him, as she had felt from his picture. He was smart and handsome and funny, and she liked his eyes. But he was also too full of himself sometimes and too hard on himself at other times. And he had very foolish notions about money and happiness. He seemed incomplete somehow, lacking the thing that would make him into what she saw in his picture. She wanted to help, to give him the thing he needed, but what could she do, a poor fugitive girl who had almost nothing and would again have to run for her life in the morning?

A thought drifted down the river of night, and she fished it out. She undid her bundle of possessions: the few poor pieces of clothing and little ornaments rigged from pretty stones. The picture of Liang. And there, the other gift from the Court Painter, a half-used box of paints that he had given her when he was trying to learn secrets to gain favor with the Princess.

Painting might help Liang find the beauty in his own life, to forget about the Court and accept who and where he was. But without a brush, the paints were useless. And would he take them from her anyway, after she had witnessed his soggy humiliation?

Just then a dream slipped silently through her window. At least, it must have been a dream. It was half man, half beast. She was afraid, yet she knew that such dreams often brought messages. "What do you want from me?" she asked.

The dream creature looked at her wistfully. "You don't happen to have a banana, do you?"

"No," she said with a tremor. "I am sorry. Please do not punish me."

The dream creature shrugged. "That's all right. I'm used to it. You were talking with Liang today."

"Ah. You hear well from your dream world."

"Actually, I hear better from a tree. 'Leavesdropping,' you might call it. Anyway, Liang didn't sound very happy about things, so I thought he might be ready to get this back." The creature held up an old scarred paintbrush. "I've kept it for seven years, ever since he threw it away."

"Are you his guardian spirit?" asked Lotus, taking the brush warily.

"No." The little human-faced monkey looked sad. "I'm just something he drew one day to pass the time."

"Then this really is a magic brush that brings things to life?"

"Yes. I drew myself a banana with it, but it tasted terrible, so I didn't draw any more, just kept it for him. He drew me some very tasty bananas before he decided I wasn't real."

"And then he just abandoned you?" She could scarcely believe this of the face from her picture.

"Don't think too badly of him. He had his dream of getting to the Court, and I was no use to him for that. Now, perhaps, he will be satisfied to stay here and I can be his friend again."

"He has not been much of a friend to you."

"He is still learning who he is. I am half a man and half a monkey; I know what it is not to fit in. In time, he will be a good person. Give him the magic brush for me."

The dream creature slipped out the window and was gone.

She sat looking into moonlight and shadows for a while, trying to understand her dream. Was the creature real? Did Liang's brush really bring pictures to life?

She used the brush and her paints to draw a June

bug on the wall. She watched it carefully. It did not move. So much for magic in the brush.

But whether the dream creature told the truth or not, she was sure that Liang would be happier if he returned to his painting. So she slipped down the path in the moonlight and tossed both brush and paints through his window.

She went back to the empty hut to wait for daylight, when she could continue her flight. "I will never see him again," she thought sadly. But it cheered her to think of the beauty he would create, thanks to her.

Not meaning to, she fell into full sleep for the first time in days and drifted softly on the river of night.

"Hey, wake up, lazybones. Look what I've got."

She shook herself awake and saw the sun was high although buried in cloud. She must be off! She bundled up her few things while Liang leaned through the window, watching impatiently.

"See? It's my magic brush! And paints! It was a gift from my father."

That stopped her. "What?"

"A gift from my father. I never knew him, but he gave me a brush when I was a little baby, which I threw away. Then he came to me in a dream last night and said, 'You have the gift. Use it well.' And when I woke up, this was in my hand. It is his gift that he has returned to me, the magic brush that brings pictures to life."

She didn't want to say anything against his father, but she was a little irritated at being left out of all this. It had seemed romantic to act as a mysterious, nameless helper, but it was actually rather annoying not to be appreciated. "It doesn't look magic to me. It looks kind of old and worn-out."

"That's all you know," he said smugly. "Here, I'll show you." And he started to paint on the wall outside her window.

"What are you doing?" she asked, but she couldn't see, so she went out the door and walked around to where he stood. The wall by the window was bare.

"I thought you painted something."

"I did."

"Where is it?"

"There," said Liang, proudly, pointing into a tree. Lotus gasped. There was a beautiful bird of silver and green, stretching its wings and preening its feathers.

"That's a very beautiful bird," she said, "but where is your painting?"

"That *is* my painting. It came to life and flew up

there, just like when I was a child."

"Stop teasing me!"

"I told you, it's the magic in the brush."

"There's no magic in that brush! I should know, because *I* returned it to you, not your father, and I tried it out first and it didn't do anything."

He looked hurt at that, and she was immediately sorry she had said it. But then his mouth twisted up and he spoke bitterly. "You're just saying that to make me feel bad. And probably to try to get something from me."

"No, I'm not. And I'm sorry I said it. What will you do with your . . . magic brush?"

"What will I do? Why, I'll use it to get money, of course. I will paint beautiful things for rich men, who will give me money when my drawings come to life. I can't paint Art, but I can paint what they like."

"You have a great talent for drawing, but I don't think you should count on it to earn money."

"Oh, you don't think I'm good enough? Well, look at this," he said smugly, holding up a tiny brass coin.

"Where did you find that?" she asked.

"I didn't find this magnificent piece of money," he replied scornfully. "It was given to me just this morning on my way over here in payment for my painting. A horse had torn its bridle and I painted a new one."

Lotus took his hand and spoke to him very sincerely. "Listen to me. You must stop making up stories and be satisfied with what you can really do. This coin that you found is the smallest in the Empire and can scarcely buy a bowl of rice."

Liang looked at it with disappointment, but shook his head. "I don't care. It's a start. And when the Guardsman tells others about my magic brush, perhaps I will get—"

"Guardsman?" she asked, her eyes round.

"Yes. It was an Imperial Guardsman for whom I painted the bridle." Lotus looked around nervously, but Liang paid her no attention. "Perhaps I will paint for other travelers and save my money and move to a bigger town, and when I'm rich enough, I shall go to Court and marry the Princess."

Lotus lost her fear in her fury. "Money! Court! The Princess! That's all you can think of! Well, I know the Court, and it's an awful place where everyone dresses in gold but lives in fear. And your Princess may be pretty, but she's the worst person I ever knew. Except, of course, for her father."

Liang nodded sarcastically. "Oh, of course. You're on very close terms with the Emperor."

"He wants to marry me!" she blurted out.

"What!"

"I was a servant to the Princess. She was always cruel to me, but I bore it for I had no family to save me and nowhere else to go. Then one day the Emperor saw me and decided he would make me his one-hundredth wife. So I ran away. . . ."

"Marry you! The Emperor! A little mud hen like you? What a liar you are!"

Lotus struck him in her fury. "Go away!" she cried. "Go away!"

"My pleasure," he snapped, "Your Highness." With a sarcastic bow, he disappeared through the bushes.

She quickly felt sorry. Her story must have sounded as crazy to him as his did to her. Except, of course, that her story was true and his wasn't. Still, their argument would always be his final memory of her and that made her sad. She took up her bundle resolutely, but she found she couldn't take the first step away from him.

Just then, there was the sound of someone in the bushes. He was returning!

"I'm sorry!" she blurted out as the bushes parted.

"That's nice," said the Imperial Guard, "but I don't think it will help much." And he snatched her up onto his horse. As she struggled uselessly, the little bundle of all she had in the world went flying into the bushes.

Liang walked along, muttering to himself and swatting at low-hanging branches with his brush. How could she be so mean? He had thought her nice, but she was like everyone else, refusing to believe him, thinking him useless and silly. Well, he *would* get to Court. Somehow.

He found himself at the riverbank, standing over the remains of his dragon. He thought a moment, then laughed. So she didn't believe him. Well, perhaps it did sound a little crazy. But not as crazy as *her* story! Well, he'd show her. He'd show them all.

He opened the paint box. Green, first, for the scales. Then gold for the belly. Then red for the claws and eyes. Mixing in darker and lighter shades to shape its roundness and the light that glinted from it. As he painted, he forgot that he wanted to startle the villagers, wanted to scare Lotus. He forgot the terror of the thing and saw only its beauty.

"There," he said, finishing, and turned to run and fetch her. But his foot was twisted in a vine. He bent to free it. It was not a vine. It was a tail of green-flashing scales that gripped him.

A great shaggy head reared up from the ground,

shaking away weeds and grass. It made short rasping sounds, as if clearing its throat. Then it shot a blast of fiery breath into the trees, and Liang forgot how beautiful it was.

With a lurch, the arch of its back heaved up out of the earth, and then its four feet with their terrible claws. The coils of the tail lifted Liang high above the ground.

The dragon shook itself like a great dog, flinging away mud and rocks. It stretched, cracking out its new knuckles and joints, pleased to be free after its years of not-quite-life. The head swung around toward the tail, and Liang was face-to-face with the red diamonds he had just painted in the center of the giant eyeballs. The dragon showed its long teeth and cleared its throat to kindle the spark for its first hot meal.

"Hey!" called a voice. "I'm hungry! Are you going to eat all of that yourself?"

The dragon stopped just short of ignition and looked around.

"I'll trade you my coconut for a bite of Artist," called the voice, and suddenly a coconut dropped onto the dragon's hard, scaly head. Dragon and Liang both looked up.

In a tree above them, a little monkey with a man's face peered down.

"Monk-Li!" cried Liang.

The dragon dropped Liang and unleashed its fire into the branches where the monkey had just been.

"I guess that means no trade," commented the monkey from the next tree.

The dragon hurried after the monkey, which leaped from tree to tree. Liang started to run toward the village but stopped abruptly.

"Monk-Li did save my life," he thought. "I can't just leave him, even if he is only a drawing. And something must be done about the dragon, no matter what." He shrugged and called out, "Monk-Li! Bring him this way!"

As he ran away from the river and village, he heard the crash of the dragon approaching and then Monk-Li dropped onto his shoulder. "I'm glad you showed up when you did," gasped Liang.

"You're welcome," said Monk-Li, although Liang had not actually thanked him. "What's your plan?"

"I don't have one yet."

"Then how about a banana? I might as well die happy."

They ran out of the trees and up a gentle slope. The dragon was taking a while to get used to its body, but it was a quick learner and not far behind.

Liang realized he had reached the foot of the

mountain. He was in a small draw with no outlet. On three sides, the sheer rock face; behind him, the dragon.

Think!

"Where do dragons live?" asked Liang.

"Anywhere they want," answered Monk-Li.

"Caves!" said Liang. In a flash, his brush was painting a wide black opening on the rock face.

"I hope this is a fast cave," Monk-Li said, looking back at the green-and-gold monster squirming its way up the draw toward them.

"I'm trying, I'm trying," said Liang. But even as he tried for speed, he couldn't help adding the stalactites and stalagmites that would make the cave a thing of beauty.

"Here it comes!" yelled Monk-Li as a spout of fire roared toward them. In the same moment, Liang grabbed him tightly and leaped into the cavern.

The dragon stopped and sniffed suspiciously at the rocks. It lapped cautiously at a little stream just inside the cave mouth. Finally, it marched happily forward. This dark, wet place was its idea of a cozy home.

Liang and Monk-Li slipped quietly from behind a stalagmite and out of the cave, hearing the happy rumblings farther inside. Liang began painting the rock back over the cave mouth. There was a roar and a rush from inside, but Liang completed the glinting crystalline faces of the granite wall, and the cave was gone.

"Is that paint fireproof?" asked the nervous Monk-Li.

Lost in the moment of creation, Liang could hardly remember what the stone wall hid. He smiled and breathed, "Doesn't it look beautiful?"

"It looks like rain. Does that paint run?" Monk-Li's worried prattle brought Liang back to himself and, without quite knowing why, he was pleased to see the little monkey.

When you've been too long in a boat, it is easy to forget the river that supports and propels you and think that the boat is the whole world. Likewise, your life can be so contained by the boat of one idea that you fail to see the river, which really carries you forward. Friendship is such a river. Ambition is such a boat.

"Where have you been all this time?"

"Well, I knew you didn't want me around, so I tried to go live with the monkeys, but they all laughed at my human accent, so I just sort of stayed in one tree or another and ate whatever I could find. And speaking of eating . . ."

"Yes, yes. But why did you risk your life for me, when I ignored you for so many years?"

"Hmm. I didn't give that any thought. You created me. I suppose I feel responsible for you." Liang laughed at that. "Of course, it should really be *you* feeling responsible for *me*," Monk-Li continued, "but you didn't, and someone ought to be responsible for someone, so I guess it was up to me. You could make up for a great deal with a banana."

"You'd forgive all my neglect for just one banana?"

"I don't know how to forgive. I just know that I'd like a banana."

Liang obliged him and Monk-Li settled happily on his shoulder. "It's starting to rain," he observed. "Where are we going? Somewhere inside, I hope."

"We're going to see Lotus."

"Ah. You want to introduce me to your . . . friend."

"No, why would I want to do that? She thinks I was bragging about my magic brush. You are going to show her that I wasn't."

But when they came to the little hut, it was empty. Liang felt more disappointed than he might have expected.

"Look," said Monk-Li, holding up something he found in the bushes. "Here's her little bundle."

Liang started to take it, then shook his head. "She is gone. I must concentrate on making money so I can get to the Court and the Princess."

He set out for the village, ready to start amassing his fortune at once. Monk-Li tied the little bundle around his waist so he could search it later for possible food and hopped back onto Liang's shoulder. "Couldn't this wait until the rain stops?" asked Monk-Li, draping the banana skin over his head like a floppy yellow hat.

Liang didn't even answer. When he reached the village, there was an unusual amount of activity. He stopped one of the farmers. "I have a magic brush that brings drawings to life. How would you like to have a beautiful bird with saffron wings and a scarlet crest? Or a sky-blue fish with fins like silken draperies? I would trade either for a bag . . . uh, two bags of rice."

But the farmer was scornful. "Liang, you are just as foolish as ever. Magic brush, indeed! Besides, what would I do with a bird or a fish except eat it? So I would be trading many meals for one meal. Pretty on the plate doesn't count for much."

Liang gestured at Monk-Li. "This is one of my paintings. And he can talk, too. Go ahead, Monk-Li. Say something. Monk-Li!"

Monk-Li looked thoughtful but said nothing.

"If your birds and fish are as ugly as your monkeys," laughed the farmer, "I certainly want none of them."

"But . . ."

"Leave me alone now. I've no time for foolishness. This rain started high in the mountains. We are going down to the river to be sure the breakwater can stand against any flooding." He and all the other villagers gathered up what poor tools they had and set out for the river, leaving Liang alone with Monk-Li.

"You ruined my plan," he said angrily. "Why wouldn't you talk?"

"He insulted me. Besides, all I could think to say was how hungry I am, and that didn't seem like a good selling point."

Liang brushed the monkey from his shoulder. "Here," he said, "I'll paint you a bunch of bananas." And he did. "That's thanks for helping me with the dragon."

"Saving your life, actually," Monk-Li thought, but was too polite to say it out loud. Besides, by then his mouth was full.

He suddenly realized that Liang was walking away from him. "Wait for me," Monk-Li called, trying to drag along the bananas.

"Stay here! You are no use to me. With my brush, I can do things that no one else in the world

60

can do, but who appreciates it? I am reduced to painting bananas for a foolish monkey. I must think of my future. Well, you have your bananas. What else do you want from me?" And he stalked angrily away.

Monk-Li looked sadly at his bananas there in the rain and, for the first time since he had been drawn, did not feel hungry.

Liang offered his paintings to several others he met, but none would listen to him. They rushed on to the river, saying the best thing he could do for them was to stay out of the way. He went home sadly through the rain, which came down heavier all the time. It was very depressing to be so remarkable and yet so unappreciated. The worst farmer in the village would be welcomed if he just brought a shovel with him.

"That's it!" he thought. "I'll make them appreciate me!" Quickly he began to paint on his favorite blank wall of the hut. As he painted, he thought of the good feel of wood in your hands and the clean heft of a well-balanced implement, and though the tools were simple and unadorned, yet they were beautiful.

The pick and the shovel fell out of the wall, and Liang grabbed them up and hurried out into the rain. He slipped and slid though the mud to the riverbank. The rain was worse than ever, and he could see only a few feet in front of him.

He stopped in shock at the bank. The river, which he had always known to be lazy and low or just a bit higher and faster in the spring runoff, had become something else. This river was not like a picture or a dream or a path. It was like a dragon, tearing blindly at all it could reach, roaring its desire to rise from its banks and sweep away the world.

And rise it would. It was already being pulled higher by countless rivulets of rain, which ran merrily to raise it from its bed. The world was mad with water.

He found the villagers near where the mountain came down to the river like a timid giant testing the water with its toe before deciding on a swim. This was the beginning of their valley, and here they had built a breakwater to protect the rice paddies from the direct force of a flood.

Liang saw Li and rushed to him. "I brought these!" he shouted over the roar of the rain, offering his pick and shovel. Li grabbed them and passed them on to the other villagers, who were scraping at the sodden earth with their hands or feeble hoes, cramming it into baskets to be added to the breakwater.

Liang had hoped for words of thanks, but it was a futile hope. "Why did you wait so long to bring these if you knew where there were tools?" the villagers said.

"You don't understand," he said, holding up his brush. "I had to paint them!"

"You wasted time painting them when you should have brought them at once?" Li shouted furiously. "You thought we needed *pretty* tools to save our rice?" He grabbed the brush away from Liang. "So, you kept this foolish stick all these years, even after you pretended to throw it away! I shall burn it when I have time. Now, do something useful for the first time in your life." He shoved the brush into his belt and Liang into the mud.

Liang's cheeks were wet with more than rain. "No one understands," he whispered as he scraped up the dirt with his hands, and he thought for a moment of Lotus.

Li was suddenly sad as he saw Liang stumbling in the dirt. "I regret that I ever pulled you from the river," he said to himself.

Then he screwed up his face and thought of their time together, of all the years since he had last spoken to a tree. "No," he said out loud in some surprise. "Foolish old man that I am, I don't regret any of it at all." He thought about that a moment, then went back to fighting the river.

The hours passed and the rain stopped, but they worked on through the night. A faint moon showed through the breaking clouds. The river ceased to rise at last, but it was still beating with great force against the breakwater. If it succeeded in eating that away, there would be nothing to turn it from swallowing the rice paddies whole. They struggled to widen and strengthen the breakwater, but the river carried it off as fast as they could build it.

Faster.

Finally, the village elders issued orders. "Stop! It is hopeless. It will all be gone in a few minutes, and then our rice will follow. We can only save our lives."

"There is nothing to be done," Li told Liang, whom he had to pull back from the narrow spit of land. "Only a mountain could stand against the river. It would take a miracle."

Liang turned to look up at the slope of the mountain. "A miracle," he repeated. "You told me once you saw something like a miracle. When you went to the fair. Tell me again."

"It was a foolish thing. This is a serious moment."

"All the serious things have been done. Why not be foolish?"

Li nodded slowly, then began to speak.

"I was a young man, then. I wanted more out of

life than the river and the rice. So I took what few things I had and left this place of my parents. I walked for many miles, seeking something better. Eventually I came to a great city, where they were having a fair. There were jugglers and magicians and . . ."

"Tell about the shooting star," said Liang.

"It was nighttime. There was a terrible loud sound, and I looked up to see a column of sparks rising into the air and then a burst of stars that disappeared as they floated out of the sky." The villagers, who had gathered to listen, looked at each other with a mixture of disbelief and awe. "A passerby laughed at me. 'Don't be afraid,' he said. 'It's just the fireworks for the fair.' He pointed to what he called 'rockets.' I knew that a place that released such powers for its amusement was no place for me. So I hurried home and never—"

"Tell me about the rockets," said Liang.

"They were red tubes of paper, with little cone-shaped hats. A piece of string came out of the other end, and it was all attached to a stick pushed into the ground. When they touched fire to the string, the fire ran up inside and the thing shot into the air with a terrible hissing sound, like a wounded snake. And then it would burst open to die in fire."

Below them, the river rushed greedily at the last

bit of earth that kept it from the rice, but Li's story had brought a strange calm upon the listeners. The world was full of terrible things—paper tubes that died flaming in the air, hungry rivers that came looking for villages. What could you do in such a world?

"Give me my brush, please," said Liang.

Li started to say no, but then he remembered that other young man who had set out to find something better before he turned back in fear. He gave Liang the brush.

Liang painted on a flat rock by the river. The villagers watched in puzzlement. "Tell me again of its death."

"It was frightening, the most terrible thing I've seen."

"And the most beautiful."

Li thought. "Yes," he said at last, "it was beautiful. Its pathway into the sky gleamed like gold, and its bursting was like the sun. And green and blue fire fell like rain."

Liang felt the beauty. He painted fire at the end of the string and stepped back. It sputtered and caught, racing up the fuse. As it disappeared inside the red tube, there was a great hissing. The spell of Li's tale was broken and everyone scattered.

The rocket lifted upward on a stream of many-colored fires. It rode high, then curved like a rainbow as it dived into the face of the mountain and exploded with a terrific blast.

In the ringing silence that followed, there was a moment's stillness, then a groaning in the earth, which could be felt before it could be heard. A part of the mountainside leaned outward in one great mass, as if yearning to leap up like the rocket. Then it came apart into stones and boulders and earth and tumbled into the river beside the break-water, broadening and extending it far into the river.

The rice paddies were saved. The village was saved.

The villagers crept out of hiding and looked at the amazing scene before them as the sun began to rise. They were finally forced to admit that there was magic in Liang's brush.

Liang knew the moment of triumph of which he had always dreamed. The thought of Lotus came unbidden. This would have shown her. He wished she were there to see.

No, he realized. He wished she were there to share.

S E V E N

"Share your dreams with me!" Liang called to the villagers. "Come, what do you want? I can paint anything to life for you." He described his bird, his dragon, his talking monkey, like a traveling merchant pitching the wonders of his miracle cure-all.

Public acclaim is like rain. In full torrent, it is overwhelming, giddy with excitement, making all bow and dance before it. But it can cease in a moment, and a day in the sun makes it vanish as if it had never been.

A village elder finally spoke. "I would like something."

"What?" Liang demanded, his exhaustion forgotten, delighted to show off.

"One of those good picks like you brought last night."

"Yes," said another, "and one of those shovels!"

They all started calling for picks and shovels then. "Can you do hoes?" someone asked, doubtfully.

"I can do anything!" Liang announced angrily. "Can't you think of more than a pick and a shovel?"

Silence, then "*Two* picks!" called a voice. "And two shovels!" called another.

"Doesn't anyone want something painted besides everyday tools? I can paint anything! Dream your wildest dream and I can make it true!"

A woman stepped forward timidly. "I'd like my *house* painted. Green, if that's possible."

"It's all such a waste," Liang was saying after several weeks of painting farm implements. "I offer them anything at all and they can only think of ordinary, everyday, boring things. And if I try to beautify them a bit, they don't like it."

Li was sympathetic, but he clearly agreed with the other villagers. "No one likes to drink milk from an orange-and-blue goat."

"I'm using up too much of my black and brown paints. I've got to vary my color scheme or I'll run out. Besides, it wasn't just the goats they objected to, it was the farm tools as well."

"Well, they had to wait so much longer when

you decided to add the carved history of the Empire to the rake handles. And if you put any weight on them, they tended to snap off around the Third Dynasty."

The villagers now thought Liang was useless in a magical sort of way. He had saved the village and outfitted it with his magic brush, but he still couldn't manage any real work in the rice paddies, which was all that counted in the end. Magic was all very well, but it didn't get the work done.

Liang's only friend was Monk-Li, but they always argued when the monkey's limited conversation turned inevitably to food requests. "Yes," Liang would say, "you may have helped me out once or twice, but that doesn't give you the right to make my life even more miserable."

He often thought of Lotus. It was strange. He understood why he had thought of her in his moment of triumph saving the village. That was just wanting to show off because she hadn't believed him. But why did he think of her when he felt bad about yelling at Monk-Li or about being stuck in this village so far from the Court? She couldn't help him, wasn't even sympathetic to what he most wanted. So why did he want to talk to her about all these things? Why did no thought feel quite complete without being told to her?

So Liang painted and brooded, and his only friend was a drawing who complained too much.

Then one day there were hoofbeats, and the same Imperial Guardsman appeared on the pathway. "You, boy!" he called haughtily. "You look familiar. Aren't you the magic boy with the paintbrush?"

Liang started to correct him, to say that he was the ordinary boy with the magic paintbrush, but decided that he probably shouldn't contradict a potential paying customer. "Yes, sir. You remember I fixed your bridle for you."

"And chattered on how you could paint anything and have it become real for money. Although what you would do with money out here I don't know."

"I *need* money, though, a lot of it. It is the only way to make my dearest wish come true."

"And what is that?"

"To go to the Court."

The Guard threw back his head and laughed. "Well, then, save your money, for I'm your fairy godmother and your wish is granted."

"What do you mean?"

"I'm here to fetch you to the Court."

Liang felt dazed. "What?"

"The Emperor called me in the other day," the

Guard said with a great air of self-importance, "to confer about his forthcoming wedding. And I told him about the magic boy and his brush, and he asked me to go and bring the paint boy along for the celebration."

The truth of the tale was that the Guard had forgotten all about the boy with his magic tricks until one night when he had had too much to drink and blurted it out in a tavern. At Court, nothing is said that doesn't get back to the Emperor's ears, and so this rather unimportant Guardsman was sent to fetch the boy. The Emperor was doubtful of the story, but the boy could entertain at the wedding by either using his truthful magic or losing his lying head. An execution always makes an occasion feel special.

"Me?" Liang asked in astonishment. "At a celebration at the Court?"

"Yes, you're to play a very important role in it." The Guard smiled.

"I shall paint whatever the Emperor wishes, beautiful clothes or exotic animals or unheard-of castles, all more beautiful than he could wish!"

"Well, that's fine. Now, you gather your things and let's be off. It's several days' ride to get there."

Liang tried to think what he had to gather, but there was only the brush and the paints. He hurried down toward the rice paddies to bid farewell to Li. On the way, he ran into Monk-Li.

"Would this be a good time to ask for a banana, or are you in one of your bad moods?"

Liang laughed and quickly drew a bunch of bananas as well as mangos, papayas, and every other kind of fruit he could think of. "Eat well," he said. "I'm off to the Court!"

Monk-Li screwed up his face in thought. "I think this would be a good time to show you what I found in Lotus' bundle. I don't know what it means, but it is a picture of you and a picture of Lotus and someone else."

Liang was pleasantly surprised that she had a picture of him, but he refused to let it show. "So she tried to paint. What's that to me? I have no time to look at her infatuated dabblings. You may keep it as a reminder when I have left for the Court."

"Aren't you going to take me?"

"To the Court? Don't be ridiculous. What use would you be to me at the Court?"

"I might remind you of who you are," Monk-Li said to himself sadly as Liang hurried off.

"Uncle Li! An Imperial Guardsman has come to take me to the Court!"

Li leaned on his rake. "I am sorry for you."

"Sorry for me? Why! It is all that I have ever wanted."

"They say there are always new and amazing things happening at Court. It sounds terrible."

"It sounds wonderful."

"You want to leave the river? Our hut and the rice paddies?" Li looked around, unable to imagine any other life.

"At the Court, they will understand beauty and appreciate what I do. Good-bye, Uncle Li. Thank you."

Li picked up his rake and hunted along its elaborately carved length until he found the story of the eighth Emperor. It was a sad story of a ruler sending his only son on a long journey from which he would never return. "He'll be back," he said to that wistful image. Just as he had with Liang, he had grown fond of the rake, even if you couldn't put too much weight on either of them.

E I G H T

Liang collapsed to the floor in wonder. The colors! The colors of the Court were more beautiful than he could have dreamed!

And more dangerous.

The Court is like a swamp. When water is not allowed its natural flow, it turns inward upon itself and eats at its own heart, rotting away beneath a surface of tranquillity. Just so, the Court seems beautiful, presenting shows of ceremony that mock the beauty and movement of real life; yet just below the surface lurk the quicksands. And the lush growth conceals the hunters and prowlers who wait to devour those lured by the beauty above into the snares beneath.

Liang was awash in the colors. They swirled around him like a whirlpool, moving, ever moving

before his dazzled eyes, yet always in the same place. Even those colors that he knew seemed transformed in impossible ways. The brown of wood was deepened and polished and shined until it needed a new name. The green of unnaturally shaped and groomed plants was lustrous with life. The water of a fishpond was so crystal clear that it put mere color to shame, even the dancing gold of a bug-eyed fish swirling its gossamer fins.

There were colors for which he knew no names, lavenders and chartreuses and fuchsias. He looked on each and felt its lineage, exactly how red and blue and yellow had wedded over generations to give birth to such a wonderful child.

The colors swirled around him and flowed over him, and he lost his breath as he breathed them in. He was drowning, but he wished never to surface again.

He was on his knees in a great room, larger than his whole village, his eyes finding in the grain of the magnificent wooden floor all the pictures he could ever imagine sketching. The distant walls were enameled in gold and scarlet, crowded with dragons and wondrous birds, flat and unmoving and unreal but colored beyond his dreams. He was dimly aware of the Guard behind him saying nervously, "Get up! Pull yourself together! Stop moan-

ing! If you get me in trouble—"

A distant double door opened and something huge came through, some great bundle or piece of furniture colored in red and gold and moved by unseen hands. No, it moved by itself, coming closer, stumping along on tiny legs, pumping stubby arms. Something like a squashed gourd perched on top, and little piggy eyes stared out at him.

Liang pressed his face against the floor. This was the most terrible person he had ever seen! He knew instinctively that only an Emperor could look this awful!

For he was a great Emperor. An imposing Emperor.

To be blunt, a fat Emperor.

They said a man could ascend the highest mountain without ever seeing the boundaries of the Empire, which were always lost beyond the curve of the earth. Just so, this Emperor, who embodied the Empire in his person, could never see his own feet for the curve of his belly. Walking was an act of faith, for his head, perched there at his personal North Pole, could never see what his legs were doing beyond the horizon.

"So this is the boy," the Emperor said, tilting his axis dangerously to regard the bundle of rags on his floor, with a combination of interest and distaste.

"Yes, Your Majesty," snapped the Guard at attention.

"Get him up so I can see him." The Guard prodded Liang with his foot. Liang rose trembling. The Emperor scrutinized him. "He doesn't look like much. Can he really do this painting trick?"

"It is not a trick," Liang blurted.

"Your Majesty," the Guard prompted, with a kick.

"Your Majesty," Liang hastily agreed. "It is my gift and I have tried to use it well, but there is little chance among farmers and peasants who have no concept of beauty. But here"—he gestured raptly at the walls around them—"here in a place of such beauty . . ." The Emperor wondered what the boy was raving about. There was no gold in this room, nothing but wood and paint. What could be beautiful about that?

"We are wasting time," he announced, waving a stubby arm at the Guard, who brought forward an easel holding sheets of parchment. Liang ran his hand in wonder over the smoothness of it, bent close to admire the silky fibers.

"Make him paint something for me! What is his specialty?"

Liang spoke excitedly before the Guard's foot could give him one of its helpful hints. "I shall paint living masterworks for you, Majesty! Creatures of radiant plumage, palaces of sky-touching spires! I shall paint your heart's desire! Imagine your most unimaginable dream and I shall create it for you. Only name it for me."

The Emperor wrinkled up his face in thought, then smiled. "Gold!" he said, with a definite nod.

"Gold," the Guard ordered, pointing to the blank surface.

Liang slowly took out his brush and dipped it into his paints and held it poised. But he did not touch the paper.

"What is the matter?" demanded the Emperor, so exasperated he accidentally spoke directly to Liang. The Guard seized the opportunity to begin creeping, respectfully, toward the nearest exit.

"I know the color gold," said Liang, "but I do not know what the thing itself looks like."

The Emperor gave a snort of impatience and snapped his fingers at the Guard, who had covered a surprising distance in a very short time. "Bring gold!" The Guard gave a sigh and a salute and slipped out.

Liang was alone with the Emperor. The Emperor, on the other hand, was completely alone, since there was only a peasant boy with him and that didn't count as anyone. Liang waited nervously. The Emperor thought of dinner. It had been almost a whole hour since he had last eaten.

At last the Guard returned, bowed, and held out a gold coin to the Emperor. The Emperor snapped, "I am quite familiar with what gold looks like. Give it to him!" The Guard saluted, executed a smart turn, and dropped it into Liang's hand.

Liang looked at it carefully. It was wonderfully shiny and heavier than he had expected. Round and smooth, with an image incised upon it. "Please, Your Majesty, whose likeness is this?"

"Mine, of course."

Liang stared in surprise from the Emperor to his golden image. "This is true Art," he said in a voice filled with awe. "I could never look at you and paint this picture." The Emperor didn't understand this statement, but took it as a compliment since that was what he was used to hearing.

Liang faced the parchment. He felt the roundness of the coin, saw the shimmer of the metal and the line of the image. He began to paint in slow, thoughtful strokes as he found the beauty of the gold.

The Emperor waited impatiently, his stubby fingers curling and rubbing together greedily as he thought of all the gold that he did not yet own. It was taking far too long. "Guard!" he exclaimed, turning away from Liang "What takes him so long when I am waiting? Is he a fool?"

"Not exactly, Your Majesty; he's an Artist," said the Guard, who felt that summed up the problem.

There was the sound of a coin striking the floor. The Guard scrambled to retrieve it and place it in the Emperor's hand. "He can't even hold on to it!" exclaimed the Emperor smugly. "Well, they say a fool and his money are soon parted. I should have known it couldn't be true. Take him and . . ."

He stopped and stared. Liang was holding out his hand. On his palm rested the coin he had been given. The Emperor looked from it to the blank canvas to the coin in his own hand.

"I painted it, Your Majesty," Liang said proudly. "Just as I told you, it became real. I can paint whatever—"

"More gold."

"Yes, I could paint more gold or I could—"

"More gold." The Emperor was drooling slightly.

Liang sighed and began to paint. The Emperor made noises of impatience, but watched closely. When there was just one brush stroke left to finish the coin, Liang instead began to paint lines below it.

"What's he doing? At this rate, it will take forever. Life is short and art takes too long."

"It's a *stack* of coins," said Liang as he put the

final touch of gold to it. The stack rounded out and cascaded at the Emperor's feet. His face changed from frown to beatific smile as he paddled his feet in the little puddle of coins. He couldn't actually *see* them beyond his personal Equator, but he could hear them clinking merrily down at the South Pole.

"More gold," he laughed happily.

"Wouldn't you like something else?" Liang suggested. "Something other than gold?"

"What else is there?" the Emperor asked, bewildered.

"Perhaps . . . jewels. Yes, jewels!" Liang quickly began to sketch a beautiful emerald necklace.

"All right, jewels, but don't worry about the decorations there, just make the stones as large as possible, and do it quickly."

"Ah, but the decoration is solid gold."

"Oh, that's all right then."

When Liang pulled the necklace free, the Emperor said, "Very nice," and tried to get back to the gold, but Liang had his own plan. Only a few minutes at the Court and he was already attempting deceit.

"Wouldn't you like to show this to someone else in your family? A wife? A . . . daughter?"

"Hmm. Yes, the Princess has been bothering me lately for pretties."

"The Princess!" thought Liang, with a shiver of joy.

"Fetch her!" the Emperor snapped at the Guard, who had again migrated to the vicinity of a door.

Left alone, Liang entertained the Emperor by painting a pile of gold, then a heap of gold, then an indeterminate mass of gold. The Emperor laughed and waded gleefully through the clinking pool that sparkled and splashed around his feet.

A woman's voice spoke behind Liang. "My father in his natural element. A pretty picture. So the boy *does* have the magic touch?"

Liang stiffened and dared not turn around, dared not breathe. The voice was not what he had imagined, but it was beautiful. With an edge, but beautiful.

The Emperor interrupted his wading for a moment. "Yes, he really is magic. And he has something for you."

Liang turned toward her with eyes cast down in a show of humility. He held out the emerald necklace.

"Ah, it is exquisite!" said the voice. Liang beamed. He raised his eyes slowly, savoring the moment.

"You have a great gift, boy," she said, smiling at him. "We will find good use for it."

Liang stared at her face. He blinked twice, then

turned to the Emperor. "Do you happen to have another daughter?" he asked.

The Princess' eyes went icy. "I am the only daughter of the Emperor's first wife. I am the Princess. Do you have any other pressing genealogical inquiries?"

Liang could think only of the Princess in the picture. He had been tricked by false beauty, betrayed by Art. His face collapsed into despair as he looked from the grotesque Emperor wading in gold to the beautiful Princess with the cruel glow in her eyes. He turned back to the parchment and began to paint. The Emperor and the Princess watched greedily.

"What is it?" asked the Emperor.

"Some sort of staff, I think," replied the Princess. "Perhaps it is magical. It has carvings along the handle."

"Why does it have a flat gray thing at the bottom?"

"I do not know."

The Guard cleared his throat. "Your Majesty, I think it is . . ."

"Yes?"

"A spade."

"A what?"

"A shovel. For turning the soil. Farmers use them."

Liang drew the shovel out of the page. He looked at it sadly. "I had only one dream, to come to the Court, to find the Princess, to create beautiful things to trade for money. My dream was a fool's dream. I was given a gift; I have not used it well. There is no more beauty in gold than in farm implements. Have a shovel instead."

The Emperor recoiled. "I want more gold."

"More jewels," the Princess interjected.

"I will paint no more gold or jewels or tools. I will not paint again at all."

"We will see about that," hissed the Emperor. "Put him in the dungeon." He waved to the Guard, who seized the unresisting Liang and took his brush away.

"No, leave him that," ordered the Emperor. "If he sees the error of his ways, he may whip up a little golden peace offering for me. He has just four days to decide whether he will decorate my wedding with his brush or with his neck in the hangman's noose. I know how to deal with Artists. I've done it before." He took a deep breath and then howled in a terrible voice, "If we can't hang the painting, we'll hang the painter!"

Liang looked up in horror. "Those words! I heard you speak them before!"

"Not very likely," sniffed the Emperor. "That was many years ago. A so-called Artist painted an insulting picture of me. It did not capture my . . . what-do-you-call-it?"

The Princess smiled cruelly. "Artistic essence. It did not capture the great ruler, the spiritual leader, the mighty warrior. In short, this portrait of His Majesty committed the unforgivable sin of actually looking like him."

"Exactly," the Emperor nodded. "But in my benevolence, I let his family accompany him . . . on the gallows." He smiled at Liang, who was frozen in horror. "It made a pretty centerpiece for my tenth wedding, the whole family hanging together like a still life. All except one baby, which, in their madness, they threw into the river."

Liang was dragged limply away, out of the colors and the light. His eyes stared sightlessly. The secret of his origin had been revealed to him and the reason for his life had been snatched away, all in one terrible moment.

He was carried down into the blackness beneath the beauty.

He had spent days in the darkness, but he dared not peep out just yet.

There are many kinds of darkness. There is the wide, echoing darkness that makes you worry what might be slithering out there in all that emptiness. There is the close, dead darkness that swallows sound whole and makes you fear that you will be next. But the worst darkness of all is that which burrows in your mind and feeds on sight and sound and, choicest delicacy of all, hope.

He was in close darkness that smelled of leather and horse sweat. There had been no movement for some time, but he was so afraid of what might lie outside his pocket of dark that he stayed there clutching his little bundle and waiting for a sign.

Suddenly, light stabbed his eyes as the flap was thrown back. "What's this in my saddlebag?"

boomed the voice of the Imperial Guardsman. "A stowaway!"

With a shriek that was chillingly human, Monk-Li scampered through a window and out of the lamplight into darkness again.

He was cramped and stiff from the days on horseback concealed in the saddlebag. He hadn't even been able to come out when Liang and the Guardsman stopped to rest for fear Liang would be angry with him.

He was glad for the darkness of night. He did not care to view the wonders of the Court and most especially did not want to be seen himself. He kept to the high places and crept and listened. He didn't care about the elaborate decoration of the Court, but it did offer good pawholds for climbing.

He peered through many windows, but found nothing to quiet his fears until suddenly he saw a beautiful, sad young woman dressed all in the finest white robes. It was Lotus! He started in, but stopped when he heard a voice. He peeked in a little further and saw a lovely but cruel-eyed woman and the fattest man he had ever seen. He knew the woman's face from the picture in the little bundle he clutched. He listened and watched.

"Why do you suppose she ran away?" asked the Emperor, staring at Lotus with the interest he usually reserved for new tidbits from the Court Chef. She kept her eyes down and remained as silent as the object the Emperor considered her to be. He walked slowly around her, as if the answer might show from a different angle.

"Perhaps she did not wish to marry you, Father," suggested the Princess with a nasty smile.

The Emperor gave a little wave of one of his extremities, which dismissed that as simply inconceivable. "A slave pass up the chance to marry an Emperor and live in luxury? No, no, it must have been something you did to her."

"I always treated her exactly as she deserved."

"And yet she fled."

"Perhaps there is someone else she loves."

"What! Who can give her more than wealth, lands, influence, dominion?"

"A handsome face, a youthful body."

The Emperor was puzzled. His little face wrinkled like an ancient apple. "There are people who prefer such things?"

"The poor are not like us."

"Poor things!" the Emperor murmured sympathetically.

"I think it would be best just to have her executed and be done with it."

Lotus swallowed hard at the Princess' casual

words, but showed no outward sign of fear.

"You're probably right," the Emperor said, agreeably, "but then I couldn't marry her. I mean, if she were dead, it wouldn't count, would it? And I have my heart set on one hundred wives."

"You could always marry someone else."

"Yes, but all the others *want* to marry me, and that takes some of the fun out of it. Perhaps we could find whoever it is she loves and execute *him*, instead. If she just loves him for what he is, once he isn't that anymore, she will stop loving him. Then she can love me for what I own."

The Princess shrugged. She didn't care who was executed as long as someone was. She was in an irritable mood, and nothing soothed her like a good execution.

"Perhaps she would like some nice jewelry," the Emperor mused. "If I could just get that magic boy to paint her up some trinkets, maybe . . ."

"Yes, Father, but he refuses to paint, so you might as well just execute him and be done with it."

The Emperor started to answer her, but a sound from Lotus made them both look at her. She was staring at them, wide-eyed.

"A boy who thinks he has a magic paintbrush?" she asked weakly. "You know of him?"

"Not exactly," said the Emperor. "This is a magic boy whose paintings come to life. But he refuses to paint anymore for me, so he's in the dungeon, straight down below us. But what's this about a magic paintbrush?"

"Your Highness," said Lotus with a low bow, "release this boy, and I will marry you willingly in three days' time as you have planned and be the best wife you ever had."

The Emperor and the Princess looked at each other. The Princess smiled wickedly. "I think we may have stumbled upon her lover. One more good reason to execute him immediately."

Lotus gasped, but looked beseechingly at the Emperor. His brow was knotted in unaccustomed mental activity. "Yes, that's two good reasons to have him killed, but if freeing him would guarantee my domestic tranquillity, perhaps I should let him go."

The Princess snorted. Lotus was pale as death, but she bowed again and said, "Thank you, my Lord."

It was then that Monk-Li made his one unfortunate effort at diplomacy. He couldn't bear the thought of this grotesque man either marrying Lotus, who had been very nice to him, or executing Liang, who had not been all that nice but had given him life and a fair number of very tasty bananas, and he thought he saw an obvious solution that would please everyone. Hopping down from the window, he made an awkward bow and addressed the astonished Emperor.

"Your Highness," he said.

"My dream creature," gasped Lotus.

"What manner of devil are you?" demanded the Emperor, cowering away from him.

"I am Monk-Li, the closest friend of Liang the Magnificent as well as living proof of his great skill. You seem to be acting under the mistaken impression that Liang himself possesses the magic. In fact, it is his paintbrush which is magic, as he himself says, and as I demonstrated once by bringing a banana to life for myself." He saw no reason to mention he couldn't eat it. Everyone had different taste in Art.

"If you just allow Lotus here to go with Liang," he continued, "I am sure he would be happy to let you use his brush yourself to paint whatever you want." Monk-Li smiled broadly, unable to see any flaw in his reasoning.

The Princess laughed. "The brush! All we need is the brush!"

"No!" shouted Lotus. "I have used the brush myself. There is no magic in it."

"Too late for lies," purred the Princess. She gestured to Monk-Li. "The Artist's work speaks for itself."

The Emperor called in a Guard. "Go to the dungeon. Take the paintbrush from the boy and bring it to me. If he resists, kill him. If he doesn't resist . . . kill him, anyway. Then take a detachment to his village and destroy everyone and everything you find. I really can't have this sort of disobedience in the Empire."

Lotus was weeping. "If he dies, you shall never have me willingly."

"Perhaps not willingly," the Emperor agreed cheerfully, "but I will still have you nonetheless."

The Guard was bowing his way out, but the Emperor stopped him. "Before you go, kill this misbegotten monstrosity."

The Guard drew his sword and swung it toward Monk-Li, who was frozen in shock at just how wrong his plan had gone. Lotus threw herself onto the Guard's arm, and the sword struck a hair's breadth away from the little monkey.

"Find him!" Lotus gasped at Monk-Li as she struggled with the Guard. "Warn him! Don't worry for me!"

The Guard threw her off and swung back, but the little monkey was out the window and gone.

Liang was idly painting a fire in one corner. He had no desire to escape; the whole world was a prison to him now, and his only concern was not to die of boredom before his execution. He had painted fabulous furnishings and robes of silken splendor out of mild curiosity, then burned them when they did not rouse him from his stupor. He had created fabulous meals, but they all tasted like fish and rice since that was the only taste he knew. Now he painted fire just to have something to stare into.

A shadow dropped between the bars of a high window. It tossed a little bundle into a corner and stood catching its breath. "Oh, hello, Monk-Li," Liang said without interest. "Would you like something to eat?"

"Yes, of course I would, but there is no time. You must escape at once. They are coming to take your brush!"

"That is too bad," Liang said. "I was going to toss it on the fire next."

"They are going to slay you!"

"Yes, I know, but they are very slow about it."

"And they are going to destroy your village!"

Liang's brow creased for a moment. "I am sorry to hear that. Li was very good to me and I could never repay him. It is unfortunate."

"You must do something!"

"Why?" asked Liang in simple bewilderment. "If I saved myself, I would just die in some other foolish way. And the village will die eventually in some flood or drought or plague. Why fight against it?"

"Because you *can*. If you can, you should."

Liang smiled sadly. He painted a banana. "Here's your next meal. Be satisfied with that."

Monk-Li was very hungry, but he had to rouse Liang somehow. He threw the banana on the fire and said, "I want more from you than just my next meal."

Liang nodded absentmindedly. "I, too, dreamed of more, but I have learned the hollowness of such dreaming, for it was all given and taken away in the same moment." He stared mildly into the fire, then held his brush in it. The flame licked at the bristles.

"Lotus!" shouted Monk-Li.

"What?" Liang drew back the brush.

"The Emperor is marrying her in three days."

Liang laughed softly. "Then she was telling the truth. Good luck to her."

Monk-Li tore at his hair in frustration. "What is wrong with you? You must save Lotus and your village and yourself!"

Liang smiled gently. "I dreamed once that I

could be important in this world, that I could use my brush to make something of myself. It all came from a picture I saw, a painting of the Princess. But it was a lie. Or 'Art,' I suppose I should say. They seem to be the same thing." He thrust the brush absentmindedly into the flame. Tiny Monk-Li leaped forward and wrestled at his hand, singeing the fur on his back.

Paying little attention, Liang continued musing. "I loved that Princess. There was something about her, something familiar and warm and comforting. But the Princess of the picture was not the true Princess, any more than the bumps beyond the window were true mountains. I should have known. Why would a Princess be standing and brushing someone else's hair?"

"I know this picture!" exclaimed Monk-Li, finally wrestling the brush from Liang's hand and leaping into the corner, his fur smoking. He tore open his bundle there and pulled out the picture. "Look!" he said. "It *is* the Princess, but she is seated. Look who stands with the hairbrush!"

Liang glanced with mild interest. "Yes, that's the one. Where on earth did you get it?" He looked closer and his gaze sharpened. His mouth dropped open and he pulled the picture closer to the fire.

"Lotus!" he shouted. "It was Lotus all along!

What a fool I've been! I was so set on my false dream that I couldn't see the reality before my eyes."

There were many footsteps in the corridor. A key clanked into the lock.

As Liang's eyes devoured the picture, his mind escaped from the darkness that had enveloped it. "That's what it's all about. Lotus. I love her, Monk-Li." The terrified little monkey was whimpering and pointing at the door. Liang laughed with joy. "Don't worry. I have a new dream. And I still have my magic brush."

The door was flung open. Three Guards stepped into the room. "Kill him," said their leader, "but don't harm the brush."

Liang dipped the brush into the fire, then swirled it before him, drawing a curtain of flames across the room. The Guards fell back in fear.

Liang stepped to the far wall and wielded his brush. He thought of freedom, of liberty. He felt all the beauty that the door he painted would open onto. He turned the latch and stepped out beneath the stars.

"Run!" urged the monkey, clinging to his shoulder. But Liang knelt down and began to paint on the path. Something large and white, a long irregular oval, with a dark tail streaming back from it.

"What is it! What is it!" chattered the monkey as the first Guard burst through the door, drew his sword, and stepped within swinging distance.

Liang stepped astride his drawing. "It is a horse as seen from above," he said, with a last stroke. A great white stallion rose up between his legs and leaped forward at full gallop as the Guard's sword flashed down through the emptiness, which had held Liang a moment before. "I don't know how to mount a horse, so it was easier to do it this way."

"Where are we going?"

"First the village, then the wedding."

"Were we invited?"

"Of course! We were told we would be the main entertainment. And so we will."

"Can we stop for food?"

"No stopping now until it is done."

Monk-Li thought sadly of the banana he had thrown into the fire.

T E N

Happy thoughts of breakfast were beginning to edge their way out of dreams
when the hoofbeats echoed through
the village, making the villagers
think of distant thunder.
Coming closer. Pulling the
storm behind it.

A thunderstorm is both blessing and curse. You
huddle behind your door and think of the good the
rain will do for the rice, while you pray that the
lightning will not strike. Or if it must, that it will
strike someone else. The thunderstorm shatters a
village into a collection of lonely people.

A galloping horse could mean nothing good.
Each villager heard and hoped that the bad news
wasn't for him or her. They huddled silently in
their beds and hoped the wail of grief would arise
at some other house.

The hoofbeats stopped, but the sound of the

alarm bell shattered the silence. This seemed strange to the villagers since there *was* no alarm bell. They peered out cautiously to see who was ringing what.

Monk-Li was ringing the freshly painted bell while Liang busied himself with other drawings. Without looking up from his brush, he spoke rapidly to the villagers, who approached slowly. "I have ridden for two days and nights to warn you! The guards will be coming soon! They will destroy the village! It is my fault and I'm sorry, but there's nothing to be done so you'll have to leave at once! I am painting weapons, which you can use to . . ." He broke off as he realized no one was doing anything. They were just standing around, listening, and watching. "Don't you understand? You will be killed, the village destroyed!"

"Where did you get a horse?" asked one of them.

"He must have succeeded at Court," a woman said to Li, who had just arrived. "I suppose he is rich."

"Yes," said Li. "It's too bad. I knew he wasn't much use, but I didn't think he'd wind up rich."

Liang shouted at them. "Gather your belongings! Leave the village! The Guards are coming!"

There were embarrassed chuckles at that. Li tried to calm him. "Where would we go if we left?

We know no other place."

"And if the Guards wish to kill us," said an elder, "what can we do? When Fate rides a horse, the man afoot might as well save on shoe leather."

There were nods of agreement at this bit of wisdom. "They have a point," said Monk-Li.

"Listen, Mother," said a little boy, "the ugly monkey said something."

As Monk-Li withdrew into a dignified silence, Li looked closely at him and said, "It's not so ugly."

"It's just imitating its betters," said the boy's mother. "That's what monkeys do. They can't think or act for themselves."

"If that's true," Liang said, bitterly, "then you're all monkeys! You're in mortal danger, yet you just stand chattering like stupid monkeys."

"I resent that," put in Monk-Li.

"He talked again," said the boy.

"He imitated again," corrected the mother.

"Take this," Liang muttered, forcing a painted sword into an unwilling hand. "And this. And this." Spears. Bows and arrows. "I won't let you just stand here and wait for death."

The villagers were awkward and embarrassed. Some held the weapons like farm tools, points dug into the ground. One man cut his hand because he grabbed the wrong end of a sword. Another carried a spear over his shoulder and bumped his neighbors with the shaft whenever he turned.

"Hold them up!" Liang shouted. "Points out! Defend yourselves! Good! Like that!" He pointed happily to the man with the bow, who had actually managed to fit an arrow and draw the string. But then he let go of the wrong thing, holding on to the string while the bow whipped back and smacked him in the eye. The arrow dropped and stuck him in the foot.

"You see," said Li, "we know nothing of these things. We could not defend ourselves and would just make the Guards angry. That would not be good."

"Is it worse to be killed by angry Guards than by happy ones?" Liang asked bitterly.

Li shrugged. "If it has to happen, it might as well be as pleasant as possible for all concerned."

"Well, there is still one weapon that stands between you and your deaths!" Liang held his brush high like a banner. A leather-clad hand whipped out and snatched it away.

"Just what we were looking for," said a Sergeant of the Imperial Guards. Liang turned to find a dozen Guardsmen with swords drawn. The villagers offered their weapons with ingratiating smiles.

"Monk-Li! Why didn't you warn me they were here?"

"I didn't like that remark about stupid monkeys."

"Mommy, the monkey imitated again."

"That's very good, son."

The Sergeant was used to dealing with peasants. Pointing with the brush, he told them where to stand and in what order they would be killed. They all complied with bows and smiles. "But first," he said, turning to Liang, "we'll finish off this one."

The Sergeant was surprised when Liang took to his heels, running off down a wooded path. "Hey! After him!"

The Guards quickly mounted their horses and plunged into the wood. "Stay here!" the Sergeant ordered the villagers as he rode off. They all nodded agreement.

The Guards could move faster, but Liang knew the woods better. He ran through the tightest places and crawled through the heaviest undergrowth. The Guards would lose him, then circle around and catch up again. Finally, he ran out of woods and was surrounded in a small draw at the foot of the mountain. There was no way to climb the sheer rock wall. He was trapped.

The Sergeant galloped up. "This will do nicely.

All right, men, draw your bows. Set your arrows and ready! Aim!—"

"Wait!" called Liang, staring at the ring of arrow points that encircled him. "Don't I get a last request?"

The Sergeant frowned. "I don't see why you would."

"It would only take a moment and wouldn't inconvenience you at all."

"Well . . . what is it?"

"I would like to paint my final resting place, a cave here in the mountain that can be my tomb."

"With this brush? Oh, no, we were warned what you could do with this."

"But you would see exactly what I am painting, and you could kill me before I could try any tricks."

"If you painted a cave, you could run off into it."

"Not if you tied a rope on me."

The Sergeant shook his head. "No, this is all very nice for you, but our orders are to get this over with as quickly as possible. Ready! Aim!"

"I can paint gold, too! A piece for every man here to make it worth your time!"

They all lowered their bows and looked at the Sergeant, who pursed his lips thoughtfully. It was a great honor to be a Guardsman, but not a high-paying one. "On the other hand," he said, "it never hurts to take humanitarian concerns into account. It improves the public image of the Guards. All right, paint away. Uh, do the gold first."

So Liang was tied at the end of a rope while he painted, and the Guards watched him down the shafts of arrows fitted to drawn bows, ready to fire at the first hint of trickery. Coins were painted and distributed after being bitten to ensure their gold content. Then Liang began to paint a cave.

"Why make it so big?" asked the Sergeant.

"I don't know," said Liang. "It just seems nicer." It had a wide, high opening, and he added stalactites and stalagmites.

"Well, hurry it up. There are a lot of other people waiting to be killed, and they're probably getting hungry. You should show some consideration for other people's feelings."

"Yes, yes, just another minute." Liang concentrated, feeling the depth and mystery of the cave, the beauty of its formations, the strength of its stone. He made the last stroke and stepped to the side of the cave mouth.

"All done."

"About time, too. All right, men. Ready! Aim! Fire!"

The last word was not a command but a statement of fact. A column of flame burst out of the cave, followed closely by the head of Liang's dragon, which was not amused at having been painted into the mountainside for so long.

The Guards dropped Liang's rope and loosed their arrows at the dragon. The points rebounded harmlessly from its scales, serving only to worsen its already bad mood. The Guards broke and fled, and the dragon came out after them.

From his place of concealment beside the cave mouth, Liang swung his rope around the dragon's neck, pulled himself astride, and tied himself tightly in place. The dragon could scarcely feel him there as it chased after the scuttling men in black. Liang twisted around and began to paint on the dragon's back.

"To horse, men!" called the Sergeant. "We can't fight it, but we can outrun it!" He had scarcely finished saying that when the dragon appeared over a tree, tentatively flapping the wings Liang had drawn. The Guardsmen took this as an auspicious moment to resign from the Imperial service. Throwing off their armor and clutching their gold coins, they jumped into the swirl of the river and disappeared far downstream.

Liang poked and prodded until he found the dragon's one point of sensitivity. Leaning forward along its neck, he seized one long-stalked ear and twisted. The dragon roared and flinched in the direction of the abused ear. Liang grabbed both ears and soon mastered the art of dragon steering. He swung the dragon back to where the villagers had gotten tired of waiting and wandered off to get a little work done before their executions. Only Li and Monk-Li were watching as the great green dragon lowered itself, flapping and snorting.

"You've been painting again, haven't you?" Li called, wagging his finger at Liang, who was wrestling to keep the dragon from setting fire to the huts.

"I always tried to get him to settle down," said Monk-Li, "but he never listened to me."

"He never listened to anyone," said Li to the little monkey. "Oh, you *do* speak our language. Well, that's nice. I'm hungry. Do you want some lunch?"

"Now you're speaking *my* language!"

"If I could interrupt for a moment," gasped Liang, stretched out on the scaly, twisting neck, "we've got a wedding to stop! Jump up here quick!"

Li looked dubiously at Monk-Li. "He must mean you."

"I'm afraid so," Monk-Li sighed as he scampered up the scaly side to reach Liang in the curve of the neck. "Why did it have to be a dragon?" he asked.

"Because I didn't think a banana would frighten

them particularly." Liang looked down at old Li with fondness and sadness. "Good-bye, Uncle Li. Whatever happens, I don't think I will be able to return here. Thank you for all you did for me. I am sorry I did not turn out better."

"You turned out to be yourself," Li said, "and I was glad to know you. Although I could have done without the Art. It was a little too exciting for an old man like me."

Liang pulled back on the dragon's ears, and they shot skyward. As the village, river, and mountain dwindled beneath them, Monk-Li asked, "Could you steer a little smoother? This is even rougher than that horse."

"No, I don't think I can, but I bet you could." Liang set the startled monkey's paws on one of the dragon's ears and wrapped his tail around the other. Then he leaned back into the crook of the dragon's neck and folded his arms happily as Monk-Li's feet clung desperately to the bony crest of the dragon's head. "That way, I think," Liang gestured languidly. "Pull a little more to the left."

"What do you plan to do when we get there?" panted Monk-Li.

Liang shrugged. "I'll figure out something."

"I feel so much better," said Monk-Li as they soared into a cloud.

Li watched them disappear into the heavens, and he thought suddenly of those long-ago rockets riding their trails of fire to the stars. For a moment, he wished he had boarded the dragon. Then he shook his head and turned back to the rice.

Lotus was making a mess of things. She tried to fix the black line above her eyes, but it continued to smear, so she spread on makeup remover and wiped it all off. She had put such face paint on the Princess a thousand times, but it was different when your own eyes stared back from the mirror. Of course, she could have let her servants apply the makeup that the Emperor demanded of his bride, but she couldn't bear being waited on. So she sent them away on made-up errands to give her time alone for thinking.

She leaned back and looked at herself in her splendid wedding robes. "What do you want?" she asked the face, which she did not know was beautiful. "You will be a wife to the Emperor until he tires of you and goes looking for number one oh one, and then you will live quietly in the Women's Quarters with your every need attended to. What more could you wish for?

"Liang," she whispered. "I could wish for Liang." She sighed and stared wistfully up at the ceiling of her chamber, which shuddered and gave way as Liang descended through it. It would have been a pleasant surprise except that he wasn't alone.

"Sorry about this," Liang puffed as he and Monk-Li wrestled with the dragon's ears. "Only way I could get here in time. Not married yet, are you?" Lotus shook her head and stepped behind her makeup table to avoid the thrashing tail.

"Good," panted Liang. "I realized . . . facing death . . . and the end of all my dreams . . . that you were all that mattered to me. I love you."

Lotus missed some of this because a writhing dragon can be a bit of a distraction. But she got most of it, and her eyes glowed between their smeared black lines. "I loved you even before I met you," she said.

At that moment, the dragon's foot found the rope that held Liang in place. A flick of a razor-sharp claw sent Liang and Monk-Li sprawling. The dragon blasted the rope into ashes with its fiery breath and swung its head about to find its former passengers pressed into a corner with nowhere to run. It stepped close, blocking any possible escape route, and made its raspy ignition sound.

Liang dipped his brush in paint and quickly made a dark little cloud on the wall. As the dragon gaped to shoot its fire, a sudden, very localized rainstorm floated down its throat and set it coughing. Liang tried to paint the mouth shut, but it was too big and bit at him before he could begin to cover it. Liang painted gaps in the teeth and slipped through them. Monk-Li tried to climb to the dragon's head, but it shook him off into a distant corner.

Liang looked away for a moment to see that the monkey was all right, and the dragon knocked the paint box from Liang's hand. He was left with a dry brush and no ideas.

"Farewell, Lotus," he called. "Try to run while he's busy with me!"

The dragon spit out the last of the storm cloud and was ready to ignite. It stretched one claw forward to pin him against the wall.

Suddenly, a little white pot came flying and shattered against the outstretched talons. "Hey, dragon!" yelled Lotus. "Try some of this!"

"No, Lotus!" Liang called. "You'll just make him mad! Run while you can!"

"You can't just fly down and say you love me and then expect me to watch calmly while a dragon eats you! Hey, dragon! Come and get it!" And she hurled another bottle from her makeup table.

Liang wondered why he wasn't dead yet. He

turned his gaze from Lotus to the dragon, which was staring down in confusion at its mighty green forelimb. But where the little white pot had struck it, the color was gone and the roundness had disappeared. Only the outline was left—just a sketch of a claw with a shocked but still very alive dragon attached to it.

"What was that stuff you threw?" inquired Liang.

"Makeup remover. Works wonders at correcting mistakes. Even big ones like that."

With a laugh, Liang whipped out his brush and dipped it into the puddle of white goop. The dragon broke from its trance and snapped its jaws toward him, but Monk-Li leaped between its ears and pulled back hard. Lotus scrambled among her things to find more remover and throw it.

Liang spread a quick brushful over the curving lines of the neck, the shading under the belly, the highlight on the back. Wherever there was roundness, the paint was wiped away and flatness remained. One claw touched the wall and remained there, a flat drawing on the rich wood panels. As the dragon squirmed to retain its third dimension, more and more of it touched the wall, settled, flattened, stuck.

Finally, there was just the twitching head. Liang

painted away the shadow of the chin, the glint of the eye, and, as Monk-Li carefully released each one, the roundness of the ears. He stepped away and looked at it then. It was twisted in agony, yet it lay perfectly flat upon the wall and was no longer alive.

"It looks just like one of the Court Painter's works now," said Lotus as she stepped beside him to admire it.

Liang was surprised. "You mean it's Art?"

"Art's not so tough," put in Monk-Li. "You just paint the life out of it."

Liang smiled and took Lotus' hand. "Come, we must be going."

She frowned. "I cannot. In a few minutes they will fetch me for the wedding. If I am not here, they will hunt me down and you as well. I fear all your trouble with the dragon has been for nothing."

"She's right," said Monk-Li.

"Who asked you?" snapped Liang, and he sat down to think.

The wedding went off as planned. The Emperor was pleased that the bride seemed more willing to obey and her "I do" came without hesitation from her ruby lips. The priest pronounced them Emperor and hundredth wife. And when he kissed her, she kissed him back.

Then, unfortunately, he raised her veil.

As Liang had painted, he had looked at Lotus, but he had thought of the Princess. The result was beautiful only on the outside, a perfect likeness of Lotus with a cold heart. This greedy creature was more than happy to keep their secret so she could marry the Emperor.

All would have gone smoothly except that she also had no skill with makeup. Her eyeliner was far too heavy. Then she used too much makeup remover. And once you start removing, it's hard to stop. That was why she wore the veil down to her nose and waited for the servants to come and lead her to the ceremony.

Which went as planned until the Emperor raised the veil and stared at that blankness above her nose where her eyes should have been.

And that was when he began screaming. First just mindless noises of horror. Then orders to his Guards. "Catch them! Hurry!"

They took their time upon the road.

Love is like a pool fed by the hot springs far down in the earth. You long to dive deep into the buoyant, nurturing warmth of it and never return to the surface. But, sweet as the water is, you must still breathe the air above, even when it chills you to the bone.

Like lazy swimmers, Liang and Lotus moved just enough to keep from sinking in each other's eyes. They talked and stole sidelong glances, and their feet slowed to a stumble. Then they laughed and trotted forward happily only to slow and turn inward again. For their only destination was each other, and the road was just an excuse for movement.

Their talk was full of things that astonished them but might seem very ordinary to someone else. "You said you love me. What did you mean?"

"That when a thought pops into my head, I don't feel it is truly mine until I can share it with you." And other such things.

Liang returned the two-sided picture to Lotus, and she was delighted to get it back, telling him how she had carried it for so many years, never thinking to meet him.

"It is strange," said Liang, "that I loved a picture and it deceived and undid me. But you loved a picture that proved to be truer than the truth."

"A picture is not just what is painted. It is also what is seen, with the eyes and with the heart, and that may be very different."

Monk-Li had no interest in Art criticism. "When do we stop for dinner?" he asked from Liang's shoulder. "I can't remember when I ate last."

"To be safe, we must put some distance between us and the Court," Liang replied, walking sideways to look at Lotus.

"At this rate," complained Monk-Li, "we should be safe in two or three years." They ignored the little monkey and, out of boredom, he climbed to the top of Liang's head and surveyed the countryside. He looked hard behind them, then leaped into a tree and looked some more.

"One thing I don't understand," said Liang. "I am no longer angry, but why did you say that you gave me the magic paintbrush and why did you say it was not magic?"

"I *did* give you the brush, which Monk-Li had brought to me. And the magic did not work for me, although Monk-Li said it worked once, badly, for him. I think I understand why. Did you ever get up from your pallet on a chilly morning and put your hand back beneath your blanket and think how nice and warm it was there?"

"Yes, and how pleasant it would be to crawl back in for a few more minutes."

"But, of course, you didn't because you are not a lazy good-for-nothing."

"Of course," Liang agreed with a laugh.

"And then, after a little while, if you touched the blanket again, it was no longer warm and inviting. It was just a blanket."

"I still might have been tempted to crawl in for a few more minutes, but what is your point?"

"Did the heat come from the blanket?"

"Of course not. The blanket merely held for a while the warmth that it got from me."

"Then why are you so sure it is the brush that holds the magic?"

Liang stopped in confusion. Before he could

speak, Monk-Li jumped back to his shoulder and tugged at his ear to be sure it was listening. "They are after us!"

"Ouch! What are you saying? Who is after us?"

"I saw Imperial Guardsmen on horses and a golden litter carried by running men."

"How many men to carry it?"

"At least thirty."

"That sounds like the Emperor."

"Quickly," said Lotus, "paint horses so we can escape."

"Horses will only delay our capture. We need to get farther away than that."

"No dragons!" said Lotus and Monk-Li together.

"No dragons," he agreed, pulling out brush and paints.

"They are coming quickly!" warned Monk-Li. "Hurry!"

Liang concentrated on the ground before him. "I must see the beauty or I can't paint it."

"But—" Lotus placed a gentle but definite hand over the monkey's mouth. They waited in silence as the first sounds of pursuit reached them along the road.

Liang began to paint on the hard-packed dust of the road. The dark brown of wood against the lighter brown of earth. He shaped the wood in long curves. He could feel how it would gracefully part the flow and let it join again behind. He painted only what could be seen, hull and mast and sail, but he could feel it all and sense how each part joined and served the whole. And it was beautiful to him.

The hull rounded up over him. The mast shot above the trees, and the wind made the sail belly out so that the boat groaned in its landlocked mooring.

"It *is* beautiful," said Lotus.

"And very useful here in the middle of the road," Monk-Li snapped. He could pick out dim figures in the approaching cloud of dust.

"Get aboard!" urged Liang, breaking from his trance. He jumped up into the boat and reached down a hand to help Lotus, but she was already climbing over the rail. Monk-Li bounded to the highest lookout. "They're almost here!" he called down.

Liang sat in the bow. "Hold my ankles!" When Lotus grabbed him, he flipped over backward so he hung precariously upside down, facing forward in front of the boat. He began to paint in the road, and blue was his color now.

The Imperial Guards were surprised to find a sleek sailing vessel blocking the way, but they pressed forward. The Emperor had promised a hundred pieces of gold to the one who brought back Liang or any substantial piece of him. Eagerly a Guardsman jumped for the stern of the boat. At that moment, the boat twitched and moved forward. The surprised Guardsman fell with a splash into a deep blue stream that bubbled up into the hole where the boat had been.

The other Guardsmen continued the pursuit, but the water was too deep to wade, and it took up the whole road. They were forced into the forest on either side and slowed to a walk.

Liang hung by his heels and painted for his life. The running stream was never more than a foot or two ahead of the racing bow of the ship. Lotus clung desperately to his ankles, while Monk-Li put himself in charge of taunting the enemy as they dropped away astern.

But Liang was running low on blue. And painting upside down was exhausting. And Lotus' hold was slipping. Only Monk-Li's supply of insults seemed inexhaustible. So when Liang saw the road ahead turning around the foot of a hill, he imagined what might be beyond it. He flung the last of the blue forward in a great splash and pulled himself up into the boat as it rounded the hill and sailed out onto the great sea that was so new-painted it was still wet.

It was a very peaceful scene. Lotus and Liang scrambled about the boat, laughing and pulling at the lines, their happiness as full to bursting as the sail above them. On the shore behind, they could see the little figures of Princess and Guardsmen and the one large blob of Emperor, but it was soon too far to hear what they might be shouting.

There was only one point of discontent in the whole scene. But it would prove disastrous.

Monk-Li was hungry.

Now this was not unusual, but this time the monkey decided to do something for himself. Liang was wrapped up in his own happiness and didn't want to hear about food, so Monk-Li quietly slipped the brush and the paints from Liang's pocket.

It took only seconds to paint a banana, which looked rather like a small yellow canoe, on the rail. He remembered the bad taste of his only other effort, but he had observed Liang's technique carefully since then and felt sure he would do better this time. When the banana dropped from the rail, he couldn't get the peel to loosen, but he was so hungry he popped it whole into his mouth. A moment later he spat it out on the deck and checked his lips for splinters. The banana tasted and chewed exactly like a piece of wood.

"Some magic!" he sneered, tossing the brush to the deck. As if alive, it bounced up and over the rail. He jumped and grabbed and almost had it but didn't, and he caught the rail with his tail as the brush splashed into the sea below him.

This was bad, he knew immediately. This wasn't being mildly irritating or saying the wrong thing. This was very bad. For a moment, he swung along the rail, following the brush as it was swept away in their wake. Finally he had to do something. "Brush overboard!" he called, and jumped into the water.

Liang pulled at a rope and the sail dropped, slowing the boat to a stop. He ran to Lotus at the stern. The tiny line of the brush was just visible far beyond the bob of Monk-Li's head. Lotus was kicking off her shoes and preparing to dive in.

"No!" he told her, "stay here and guide me! I won't be able to see it when I'm in the water." He dived in and swam as best he could. He had never been a strong swimmer, but he couldn't worry about that now.

Lotus called, "More left!" or "More right!" and he kept swimming until he thought he could swim no more. Then she called, "Right there!" and he stopped to look around.

There was Monk-Li thrashing in the water a few feet away.

"Where's the brush?" Liang called out.

"It's much farther. Save Monk-Li. I don't think he can swim."

"Can you swim?" Liang gasped at the monkey, who gave a twisted grin but couldn't stop thrashing long enough to catch breath for an answer. "I'll get you on the way back," Liang snapped, and continued to swim.

Behind him, Liang tried not to hear the splashing and the gasp of "I'm sorry" and then, very faintly, "Thank you . . . for my life." Then there was only silence behind him as he swam steadily away.

Lotus watched with horror as Liang left the fading circle of ripples behind. She pulled from her belt the picture she had carried for so long and studied the face there.

"My true friend could not let Monk-Li die," she whispered and looked up. Liang was nearing the brush. A tear rolled down Lotus' cheek. She crumpled the paper in her hands.

Without breaking the faltering rhythm of his stroke, Liang turned away from the brush and swam back.

"Right there!" called Lotus, and he dived down and felt about until his lungs were ready to burst. But when he broke the surface, there was a tiny bundle of sopping fur clinging to his back.

He was exhausted and failing quickly, and the tiny monkey was now an unbearable weight. But he could see Lotus standing in the boat. She was so much more real and important than the brush he had left behind. Even as his strokes failed and his arms cramped, she filled his eyes and his heart and he knew no regret. He gave a last kick and rolled onto his back, lifting Monk-Li high in one hand.

"Save him!" he gasped, and sank beneath the waves he had painted.

Then she was in the water with a rope, hauling him up onto the deck. "I knew you would save him," she said, holding Monk-Li upside down to drain the water from him.

"I am sorry I lost your brush," said the monkey when he could speak, "but your paint box is still here."

"It doesn't matter," answered Liang, "as long as you are all right."

"I thought I was just a drawing to you," Monk-Li said.

"I thought so, too," Liang replied. "But if you were gone, who would truly savor my painting? I was no good as farmer or inventor or courtier, but I could always paint a good bit of fruit."

"Delicious," Monk-Li agreed.

Lotus let loose the bit of paper she still clutched, and it blew into the water.

"Should I get it for you?" Liang asked, wobbling to his feet.

"No," said Lotus, "I no longer need it. It was just a copy, and now I know I have the original." And she kissed him.

Liang set Monk-Li upon his shoulder and hugged Lotus to him tightly. Then they returned to sailing the little ship, their eyes fixed before them. If they had looked back, they might have seen the Emperor abruptly stop shaking his fist and calling down curses as Liang's brush fell from the sky and landed at his feet.

T W E L V E

The brush had been snatched up greedily by a big eagle. The traces of banana-yellow paint had washed out of the brush and made a shape on the water fishy enough to fool even an eagle eye. The great bird soared up and over the shore as it realized it held a stick in its claws instead of a fat fish. For a moment, its eye was caught by the bright figure jumping up and down on the shore. But it was far too large to carry, so the eagle gave a shriek of disgust and dropped the brush as it turned back over the sea.

Magic is like a wave. It has its own purpose and goal, and if you catch it right, you will have a fine ride and might foolishly think it carried you where you wanted to go. But in truth it obeys no one and goes where it wishes, drowning deep all that try to stand against it.

"The magic brush!" exclaimed the Emperor, the great globe of his body quaking with pleasure. A

Guardsman thrust it into his hand, and he held it high in triumph. "Bring me paints!" he commanded.

All the Guardsmen lowered their heads fearfully, for paints were not part of their standard field issue. The Emperor, furious, ordered their immediate execution, then got more angry because there was no one else to carry out the order. The Princess smiled and produced a paint box she had brought in case it might be needed.

The Emperor held the brush over the paints, then hesitated. At another time, gold would have been all he cared for, but he longed even more to punish Liang for introducing unauthorized bodies of water into his Empire. Greed was powerful, but bloodlust won out.

He looked out over the water at the sail disappearing into the distance. What to paint? He decided an opposite shoreline would keep them from sailing away before he could paint his own ship with which to catch them, a bigger ship, with lots of gold trim. He made a big blue upside-down "V," which was meant to be a mountain on the distant shore. He was surprised when it went racing off across the calm surface of the sea and made it shiver.

"Well done, Father! Your painted waves will swamp the boat!"

"Waves?" he thought. But he didn't want to admit that he had attempted something else, so he just painted more mountains and they were all waves. And they all raced off toward that distant sail.

He laughed horribly. "I'll burn their boat!" he thought, but wasn't sure how to do flames, so he painted smoke billowing up from the little vessel. Suddenly, a lightning bolt leaped out of the blob of smoke.

"Well done, Father! Storm clouds will bring rain and swamp them all the faster!"

"Storm clouds?" thought the Emperor. "I am even more talented than I thought." The black thunderheads boiled up to cover the sun, and rain began to pour down in sheets. The Emperor climbed into his litter so he could watch from cover. The Princess stood just outside and held the white silk draperies open for him. She was enjoying it too much to be bothered by the rain. Their eyes lit up as flashes of lightning showed the little boat foundering in the storm.

"Finish them!" she snarled. "Paint a lightning bolt just above the mast!"

The Emperor laughed. He enjoyed frustrating his daughter. "Let them have a few more moments of desperation while I paint my gold. Great heaps of beautiful gold while I watch them dying!" He began to paint upon the silken walls. A bare golden outline of piles and mounds that twisted all around the inside of the litter. And every brush stroke was filled with his lust and his hate.

The Emperor cackled in glee as he encircled himself with coils of gold. A touch of the brush finished his painting, and he reached out to catch the cascade of gold. The golden mass rounded out and became real, but still it hung on the walls. For a moment it was still, then it began to move, to . . . crawl about the litter.

The Emperor pulled his hand away. "It is so cold! What have I drawn?"

From amidst the writhing coils, a great triangular head rose up and fixed him with an icy stare. A tongue the length of his arm flicked out to touch his face. He tried to run, as much as he could, but he had surrounded himself with his own destruction and it quickly tightened about him. It was amazing to think of something as big as the Emperor being just a mouthful, but the golden jaws stretched wider and wider until he became just that.

The Princess jumped away, and the Guardsmen watched in horror as the giant serpent with the Imperial bulge in its middle slithered out and into the sea.

The Princess laughed at the sight, then climbed into the empty litter and fetched the brush. "This magic is not as simple as it looked," she thought. "We must save this Liang or it will be useless."

She began painting a boat, a large one, big enough to ride out the storm. She was careful not to make it look like anything else but a boat. When it was finished, she ordered the Guardsmen onto the deck first to be sure it was nothing but a ship.

"As the Empress commands," said the Captain.

"Empress," she said to herself, happily, as she boarded and the ship pulled into the storm, heading toward the distant sail low in the water.

"Keep bailing!" gasped Lotus, using cloth to push water over the side. Immediately more crashed in to take its place.

"It's no use," said Liang. "If only I had the magic brush."

Monk-Li scooped water in a handkerchief and said nothing.

Lotus turned on Liang. "I told you before and you didn't believe me, but there was no magic in that brush!"

"Why do you say that? It was my only gift from my father. Why do you wish to hurt me?"

"The gift your father gave you was his love for you and his love for beauty. The brush was just a tool."

"Then how did things come to life if there was no magic?"

"The magic is in *you*, not the brush. Oh, it can rub off on the brush for a while, like the warmth you leave behind in a blanket. But it is a wild, uncontrollable magic without your feeling for the beauty of what you paint. That's why Monk-Li could use it fresh from your hand to paint something that looked like a banana but wasn't. That's why it didn't work for me after so long away from your touch. The magic is in *you*, in your talent, and who can say where that comes from? And talent is a gift you must use well, or it will be taken from you."

Liang looked into her eyes, then turned away. "I am sorry," he said, "but I can't believe you." And he looked beyond the raging waves to a sail visible in the distance.

"There's a problem down below," said the Captain of the Guard.

"I don't care about down below," snapped the Princess, peering through the downpour at the little boat.

"Evidently," the Captain replied. "Neverthe-less—"

"Well, what is it, what's down below?"

"There's nothing down below."

"Then what's the problem?"

"There's nothing down below."

"Nothing?" asked the Princess.

"Nothing. Nothing below the water line. Except water."

"What do I know about boats?" the Princess mumbled to herself. "I painted what I have seen. I don't know what a ship's bottom looks like." She turned back to the Captain. "So we're taking on water?"

"We practically *are* water."

The Princess tried to look regal, but she failed. "What do you suggest we do?" she asked indeci-sively.

"Land!" the Captain screamed, forgetting a life-time of training. "Can you draw us some dirt with-out destroying us all?"

Dipping his tail in the yellow paint, Monk-Li began to add another coat to his wooden banana as he stood in the water that washed freely over the deck. "Why are you wasting your last bit of time?" Liang asked him, trying to avoid further argument with Lotus in the moments they had left.

"You have created many paintings, but I have made only two. I care about this even if I can't eat it."

Liang looked at it. "It's not well drawn."

"I still care about it."

"Here," said Liang, grabbing the monkey, dipping his tail in the black paint, and making quick strokes, adding bruises, roundness, shading. "That's what a banana looks like."

And indeed it looked very real now. Liang turned to Lotus and rapped the banana against the rail. There was the sound of wood striking wood. "See? Still just painted wood. No magic there."

"Why is it so ugly?" asked the Captain as the ship wallowed toward the island the Princess had drawn.

"Who cares what it looks like as long as it serves our purpose?" the Princess snarled back at him. "One more comment and I shall have you executed for insolence!"

"But it's all scaly and green," he said as the ship scraped to a halt on the island. "It looks like . . ."

"It *looks* like a banana," agreed Lotus, "but it's not beautiful. Do you really see it, do you really care for it?"

Liang looked at it and thought about bananas.

No, about this particular banana. With the rain driving and the waves breaking, he felt the smoothness of its skin, the sweetness of its flesh, the miracle of its individual creation within all the possibility of the world.

The beauty of it.

He raised the monkey's tail and made a quick stroke.

The island opened its monstrous eyes and twitched its hideous scales. "You fool!" screamed the Captain at the Princess.

"That does it!" she shouted, and began issuing orders for his execution. This made her feel better, even as the monster opened its gigantic mouth and she and the whole ship slid smoothly down its gullet.

"Now that's beautiful," said Lotus. She peeled the banana and Monk-Li popped the sweet flesh into his mouth.

"I've been a fool," said Liang. Lotus smiled and nodded. "But I was afraid. As long as the magic was in the brush, I was still an ordinary person. But if the magic is in me, then what am I to do?"

"It is your gift. Use it well."

Liang nodded. Then he grabbed paint box and

monkey and sprang up the mast.

He stood atop the sail and dipped the monkey's tail in the paints. "Here's the only gold a man truly needs," he said as he splashed paint on a low, dark cloud to make a glorious sunburst. Shading his eyes, he painted around it a sunset sky of gold and red and purple.

"It's too early for sundown," observed Monk-Li, squinting critically over his shoulder to see what use was being made of his tail.

"I can't do an ordinary sky," Liang said with a laugh. "I'm out of blue."

The rain stopped. The clouds cleared. The waves calmed.

Liang climbed down to Lotus, who held him close and forgave him before he could ask.

Monk-Li sat at the lookout and used his tail with its residue of paint and magic to draw unlikely roses on the mast. They showered down onto the deck and into the sea. The happy couple below did not notice the hollow thunk of their fall.

The boat rode sweetly into the painted sunset, wooden flowers bobbing brightly in its wake.

Magic is not as complicated as it looks.

We are all given a talent, an astonishing thing that we do better than anyone else. When we look each at our own gift, it seems ordinary because it comes to us too easily. But when we look at someone else's, such a thing seems inconceivable and so we call it magic.

There is magic in painting and in growing rice. There is magic in singing and in raising a child and in being a friend. There is magic in telling a tale.

Magic is a gift and cannot be acquired no matter how much effort or money or time is spent on it. Yet there is nothing wonderful about simply owning a gift. It is wonderful only in its use.

Our task, our joy, is to recognize our seed of magic and to nurture it, practice it, work it, and grow it to full bloom.

Once we have the gift, we cannot give it away or trade it for something else or sell it for any amount of money.

We can only accept the gift and use it.

Use it well.